# SiGNS of Love

This book belongs to

Cynthia
Canfield

# SiGNS of Love

# love match

Melody James

**SIMON AND SCHUSTER**

First published in Great Britain in 2012 by Simon and Schuster UK Ltd
A CBS COMPANY

1 3 5 7 9 10 8 6 4 2

Simon & Schuster UK Ltd
1st Floor, 222 Gray's Inn Road
London
WC1X 8HB

Simon & Schuster Australia, Sydney
Simon & Schuster India, New Delhi

A CIP catalogue record for this book
is available from the British Library.

PB ISBN 978-1-47111-626-1
ebook ISBN 978-0-85707-323-5

Printed and bound by CPI Group (UK) Ltd, Croydon, CR0 4YY

www.simonandschuster.co.uk
www.simonandschuster.com.au

With thanks to Kate Cary

# 1

'Thank you *so* much!' I gasp, smiling at the cheering crowd.

They go quiet and I squint against the lights, leaning towards the microphone. 'You might not know this, but I've actually been reporting the news since I was six years old.' My award – a cast-iron quill and ink-bottle – is so heavy I have to rest it on the podium. 'When Tommy Mulholland kissed Britney Jones on the swings, the rest of the playground heard it from me first.'

Below me, in the front row of the huge auditorium, Mum starts to laugh.

'But *truth* has always been my guiding light, so when Britney returned the kiss with a punch, I reported that too.'

Now everyone's laughing.

'Since then I've tried to pursue truth to every corner of the globe, giving voices to the voiceless, hope to the hopeless, help to the helpless and strength to the – er – weak.'

I can see Dad next to Mum, his face shining with pride.

'Thanks, Mum and Dad, for your faith and support. And . . .' – my throat tightens – '. . . my dear brother Ben. Your courage and spirit have been my inspiration.'

He's smiling broadly. That's worth more than any award.

Tears well in my eyes and I cover my face with my hands. The auditorium fills with the sound of shuffling. I peer through my fingers; the audience are on their feet. And now they're clapping again! Applause washes over me like a wave.

'Gemma! Gemma!' They're calling my name.

'And a massive thank you to all of you, my dear readers.' I gulp back a sob. 'Without your support, I wouldn't be standing here today.' I pick up my award and hold it aloft. Suddenly it's as light as a feather. 'And to everyone at the Oxford English Dictionary,' I continue, on a roll now, 'thank you so much for your wonderful words. And to the makers of Bic biros – thank you for your . . . your ink. And Filofax for keeping me organised and Canon for my printer and Microsoft for Office and—'

'Gemma! Gemma!'

Their shouts get louder. I feel like Brangelina and Prince Harry rolled into one.

'Hey, Gemma! What's up?'

*Treacle?*

I turn, jerked from my fantasy. The audience dissolves

into a row of wheelie bins and the award in my hand morphs into a bottle of Sprite. I'm back on Furniss Street, heading for school and my best friend Treacle is racing along the pavement towards me, her huge sports bag scuffing the ground behind her.

'What were you doing with that bottle?' Treacle reaches me and slings her bag back over her shoulder. Her real name is Tracy, but ever since I can remember everyone has called her Treacle because of her shiny black hair. 'I was watching you from the bus – you were holding it in the air like it was the Olympic torch or something.'

My cheeks start to burn and I stuff the Sprite back into my bag. 'Nothing, I was just – just – doing a bit of a workout.'

Treacle snorts with laughter. 'A workout? With a bottle of Sprite?'

'Yes, actually.' My imagination whirs into action. 'Working out with bottled drinks is all the rage right now among celebs. It's called Fizzical Education.' I shoot Treacle a sideways glance. 'That's fizz as in fizzy drink – and the bonus is you get instant refreshment the minute you finish.'

Treacle rolls her eyes at me. 'Yeah, right. You were doing your acceptance speech again, weren't you?'

I grin and nod sheepishly. The trouble with Treacle is she knows me too well.

She hooks her arm through mine as the school gates loom into view. 'I swear you do most of your living inside your head.'

'Yes, but it's way more fun in there.' I lurch forward as a Year Eleven pushes past us into the playground. 'Being a Year Nine is not easy. It should be called Year Nobody.'

Treacle frowns. 'What do you mean?'

'Well, that's how you're made to feel. Like a big fat nobody. You're not in the top year, not in the bottom. Not doing GCSEs, not allowed to work in the tuck shop. It's like we might as well not even exist. Year Nine sucks!'

Treacle shrugs. 'I like it.'

'Yeah, well,' I sniff. 'You like *football*!'

Treacle groans. 'Don't mention football. Our next match is on Thursday. I'm so nervous.'

'Why?' I look at her like she's nuts. 'You haven't lost a single game all season.'

'Yes, in the League, but this is the *Cup*. There's way more at stake!' Treacle shifts her sports bag to her other shoulder. 'Hey, isn't it your webthingy meeting today?'

'Webzine. Yep.' I feel a shiver of excitement. Mr Harris, our English teacher, has asked any students with an interest in journalism to come to a meeting after school today. He wants us to set up an online magazine for the school. This could be the beginning of my brilliant career. This could be the first rung on the ladder that leads to me breaking down in tears at an awards ceremony. This could be—

Treacle nudges me. 'Look. What's up with Savannah?'

I follow her gaze to a spot opposite the old brick bike shed. Savannah's standing there, waving at us like she's guiding a plane in to land.

By the time we get to her she's practically hopping up and down. 'Girls, I need advice!' As always, Savannah's hair and make-up are flawless, but her deep brown eyes are clouded with worry and a tiny frown is crinkling her spotless forehead. 'And I know I can trust you.'

I try not to look shocked – Savannah is normally the walking definition of cool. In all our years of friendship she has never once asked Treacle or me for advice. On anything. 'What's wrong?'

'Marcus and Josh have both asked me out,' Savannah squeals. 'What should I do? Which one should I choose?'

'Oh.' I dump my book bag on the ground. 'Marcus?'

Savannah screws up her face. 'Josh is way better looking.'

'But Marcus is *nice*,' I point out. She was going to have to talk to him as well as kiss him, surely?

'Why not date both of them at once?' Treacle suggests. '*Then* decide.'

Savannah stares like Treacle's just told her to go out with a Year Seven. 'I couldn't do that! They'd think I was some kind of date junkie.'

Treacle's the first to point out the obvious. 'I'm afraid you're asking the wrong people, Savannah. We're not exactly dating experts.' She sighs. 'If *only*.'

'Oh!' Savannah leans forward. 'Have you got your eye on someone, Treacle?'

Treacle shifts her feet and blushes. 'No.'

'Yes you have, I can tell. Come on, you can tell me. I might be able to help.'

'Well, I kind of like Jeff Simpson,' Treacle mumbles.

I wrap my arm round Treacle's shoulders and give her an encouraging squeeze. She's been madly in love with Jeff Simpson since we started at Green Park High. Sadly, like all the greatest love stories, it is tragically unrequited.

'The Year Ten football captain?' Savannah breaks into a smile. 'Aiming high! I like it. But why haven't you told me before?'

'Cos it's dumb,' Treacle shrugs. 'He's in Year Ten – he'd never notice me.'

'So?' Savannah starts pulling her gleaming chestnut hair back into a loose ponytail. 'He's a *boy*. They're not exactly complicated however old they are. Now, what am I going to do about Marcus and Josh?' She blows a stray hair from her lips and looks thoughtful. 'Josh,' she decides. 'He *is* better looking.'

A shout goes up from across the yard. A huddle of boys are pointing at a couple ducking out from behind the bike shed.

'Could they look any smugger?' Savannah sniffs as Pete Croft and Laura Parkes emerge into the sunshine, hand in hand. But I can't help smiling as I watch Pete offer to carry Laura's schoolbag. They've been going out for over a year now, which is practically marital status at Green Park High. It's been sweet watching their relationship blossom and grow. But I don't know what they will do if the Head sticks to his plan of demolishing the old shed and putting up shiny new bike racks. There'll be nowhere left for sneaky snogging sessions.

An idea for my first webzine article explodes into my head like a camera flash. Pete and Laura aren't the only ones to use the shed as cover for a bit of break-time one-on-one. Everyone's dating activities will be seriously curtailed if the shed is destroyed.

OMG! I can just see the headline now.

*SOS! Save Our Shed!*

And with one well-written article, I could spearhead a campaign to save the old building. And bring back hope to the hopeless and love to the—

A flying football stings my legs. 'Hey!'

As it bounces away, Treacle stops it neatly with her foot.

Savannah's smiling. 'Look who's coming to get his ball back,' she whispers.

Treacle looks up as Jeff Simpson skids to a stop beside us.

'Sorry,' he grunts. 'Ball got away from me.'

Treacle hooks her toe under the ball and flicks it up to his chest.

'Nice.' Jeff knocks the ball down, catches it on his foot and balances it there.

'Yeah, uh, you too,' Treacle mutters.

'Thanks.' He lofts the ball then plays keepie-uppies for a moment before lobbing it back towards Treacle. She catches it on her foot and deftly kicks it back to him. It's like watching one of those nature programmes on TV. I can just hear the voice-over in my head. *We are now witnessing the dating ritual of the football fanatic, who like to woo each other with their fancy footwork and dribbling techniques.*

Jeff cocks his head and looks at Treacle. 'Impressive.'

I can see Treacle heading for a blush and prepare to cut in. But Jeff's still talking.

'We could use someone like you on our team.' He bends and picks up the ball. 'Shame you're not a boy.'

As he turns and heads away, Treacle stares after him. 'He wishes I was a *boy*!' she wails.

'At least he's noticed that you're a girl . . .' I say, trying to be encouraging.

Savannah picks up her bag. 'He'll work it out eventually.' She breezes away towards the entrance. 'They usually do.'

'In the early 1600s, German astronomer Johannes *blah* mathematically analysed known astronomical *blah* in order to develop three laws to describe the motion of planets about the *blah* ...' Mrs Murray's voice drones over the classroom. Beside me, Treacle yawns. I pick up my pen.

*The Head wants to demolish the bike shed. He says bike racks will add more space to the playground. But what sort of space?*

'Of course, Newton tells us that the magnitude of the *blah* is in inverse proportion to the square of the distance from the *blah*.'

I hardly hear Mrs Murray.

*Public space, that's what.*

This article's going to rock.

Snogging is not a spectator sport. People need privacy not prying eyes.

Mrs Murray turns and starts writing on the white-board. My pen is flying across my jotter.

*No one would build a staffroom with glass walls. Take away our shed and you take away our right to romance.*

The bell rings.

'For homework,' Mrs Murray calls as the class begins scraping back its stools, 'read chapter *blah*.'

I slide my jotter into my bag at breakneck speed. 'I'm off to the webzine meeting,' I say to Treacle. 'Wish me luck.'

'You won't need luck,' she replies. 'You're a brilliant writer. You're going to knock 'em dead.'

I smile at her and not for the first time feel massively relieved that she is my best friend. 'Well, if I do ever make it as a journalist, I'd better get the exclusive interview with you when you become captain of the England women's football team.'

Treacle high-fives me. 'You bet.'

I jump to my feet, nearly tipping my chair over, and make my way to the door.

'Don't forget to phone me to let me know how it goes!' Treacle calls after me.

'OK!' I charge out of the classroom and mount the stairs two at a time. There is no way I am going to be late for this meeting. My whole future in journalism could depend on it.

The old storeroom that has been appointed the webzine HQ is over on the other side of the building. So by the time I arrive I'm red-faced and breathless. The musty smell of damp hits my nose as soon as I open the door.

Mr Harris is sitting on a chair by the door, cleaning his glasses with his tea-stained tie. As always, his curly black hair is sprouting from his head like telephone wires. He looks at me and smiles. 'Hello, Gemma.'

'Hello,' I pant back at him. Then I see Cindy Jensen sitting at a desk at the head of the room, a pen poised in her perfectly manicured hand.

'Glad you could come,' she says in the least 'glad' voice I have ever heard in my life. She jots something on the clipboard in front of her. Blonde, icy and a year above me, it seems she's already taken control of the meeting. My heart sinks. I hope there will be other people from my year coming.

The door squeaks behind me. I turn and see Jeff Simpson walk in. Oh my God. This is a brilliant development. If Jeff is going to be working on the webzine I'll have plenty of opportunity to get to know him better. And if I can get to know him better then I'll be able to pass on vital information to Treacle, like whether or not he's single and what he likes to do other than football.

And I'll be able to make him see that Treacle is an even better match for him than the Cup Final.

Jeff squeezes past me and takes a seat beside Mr Harris. The room's cluttered with unwanted tables piled high with tattered textbooks.

'Thank you for coming, Jeff,' Mr Harris says.

Jeff sighs and mumbles something about not having a choice.

'We'll get those English grades back up in no time,' Mr Harris continues, oblivious.

So Jeff is here as some kind of punishment. My initial excitement starts to fade. If he doesn't *want* to be here, he may not talk much and I'll never find out any juicy titbits for Treacle.

I look for a space to sit. Mr Harris, Jeff and Cindy are using all the chairs that aren't stacked behind the table clutter. I spot a stool between two old desks and sit down, realising too late it's only about half a metre high and I'm sitting so low I can hardly see over the stacks of Jane Austens and GCSE maths textbooks towering either side of me.

The door opens and Will Bold saunters in as if he's a rock

star who has just parked his motorbike in the hall. *Another Year Ten*. I hug my schoolbag and wish for a Year Nine to arrive. I really don't want to be the youngest one here.

Will pushes his hand through his dark tousled hair and it falls into place like it's straight from a shampoo ad. How does it do that? My hair will look like it's starting its own ecosystem by now. No matter how long I spend with the straighteners before breakfast, by the end of school, the curls are back and crowding my face like kids round a chip shop.

I try to imagine my curly hair away. I try to picture myself with perfect straight hair like Savannah. I can't do it. I'm going to die unkissed. After all, what boy wants to be seen with a girl who can go from babe to yeti in less than three hours?

Will looks down at Cindy. His gaze stops at her clipboard. 'Taking names and numbers already?' he asks.

'There's nothing wrong with being organised,' she retorts.

Will laughs. 'That what all dictators say.' He heaves a chair from behind one of the tables and sits down.

'Gemma?' Mr Harris beckons to me. 'You look like you'd be more comfortable on one of these.' He drags a chair from a stack and puts it beside Will's. 'You'll get a better view from here.'

I blush as I slide out carefully from between the textbooks. I'm not sure I want a better view if it means sitting so close to Will. I knock the pile of Austens. It totters dangerously till I slap my hand on the top copy. 'Oops.' A grin freezes on my face. No one comments, but Mr Harris smiles at me encouragingly. I cross the room, really envying the Invisible Man.

Jeff's busy picking a bit of dried mud off his shoe. Cindy's eyeing me like she's watching a toddler bash the square block against a triangular hole. I don't even look at Will, but I *feel* his gaze as I take my seat. Then he speaks.

'A Year Nine?' He sounds surprised. 'Got a name?'

'You may find this shocking, Will, but *all* Year Nines have names.' A new voice makes me jump. Sam Baynham – lead singer of the best band in the school and another Year Ten – is standing in the doorway. He flicks his shaggy blond hair away from his face and smiles at me. A small silver earring glints in his left ear. 'You're friends with Savannah, right?'

I slide my bag to the floor, then feel naked without it and drag it back on to my lap. 'Yes. G-Gemma,' I stutter. Savannah's so cool, everyone knows who she is. I wish she were here right now.

Cindy's face has turned from ice queen to cheerleader. She's beaming. 'So glad you could join us, Sam.' And she sounds like she actually means it this time. She points at a pile of chairs. 'Grab a seat.'

As Sam makes himself at home, I stare hopefully at the door, leaning forward as it opens.

Phillip and David Senior walk in. Identical twins. Identically nerdy. And identically in Year Ten. I slump back. This time when the door opens, I don't even bother to move.

Barbara Tweed walks in. Barbara is Cindy's best friend and, surprise, surprise, *another* Year Ten. Her blue eyes look like saucers behind her super-thick glasses, and her mousey hair is twisted into two uneven plaits. No one knows why über-babe Cindy Jensen is best friends with a sweet but undeniably fashion-challenged geek like Barbara Tweed. Savannah reckons that Cindy likes to hang out with someone who makes her look pretty. Treacle says that's a dumb explanation – Cindy doesn't *need* help looking pretty. Her theory is that Cindy likes having someone she can boss about. I just think they've been friends since *way* before it mattered who's cool and who's pretty; that's a bond even high school can't break.

As Mr Harris grabs a chair for Barbara, Cindy looks at her watch. 'I guess that's everyone then.'

*Everyone?* Did I get it wrong? Were people outside Year Ten even invited? I try to picture the flyer on the English Department noticeboard. It's red. It says *WEBZINE* in big letters at the top. I feel sweat form icy beads on my forehead as I try to remember the wording underneath. *Storeroom. Wednesday. 3.45 pm. Email Cindy Jensen if you need more details.* But what else did it say? *Everyone welcome?* Or was it *Year Tens only?* My heart's racing. Maybe it didn't need to say Year Tens only. Maybe, if I'd bothered to email Cindy, I would have found out. Duh! Why am I so dumb? I clutch my bag closer to my chest. I shouldn't be here. It's obvious. I feel like an idiot. Why did I assume I—

Mr Harris stands up. My stampeding thoughts skid to a halt.

'OK, well, thank you all for coming and welcome to the very first meeting for the brand-new Green Park High webzine. Now, as you all know, Year Eleven are all a bit preoccupied with their GCSE work right now, but it's great to see so many here from Year Ten.' Then he smiles at me. 'It's a shame we have no Year Eights, but at least we have one Year Nine to represent the younger voice of the school.'

I feel torn between relief and irritation. *The younger voice?* Thanks, Mr H.

'Thank you, Cindy, for suggesting we start this webzine.' He nods at her warmly before continuing. 'I think it's very important that this publication feels *owned* by you, the Green Park students, so I'm going to be stepping back now. If you need anything, I'm here, but really I'm just your point of contact as a member of staff. This is *your* magazine. And this is your new head-quarters.' He looks around the cluttered storeroom sheepishly. 'The caretaker will be clearing it up for you this week – bringing in some computers and suchlike. But anyway, that's enough from me . . .'

He gestures towards Cindy as he sits back down.

She's on her feet and in front of her desk in the blink of an eye, clipboard in hand. 'Thank you, Mr Harris. Since this webzine was *my* idea,' she announces, 'and because of my father's background in journalism, it seems sensible that I should be editor-in-chief. Clearly, I have more experience than the rest of you.'

'Experience in what?' Will flashes her a look from under his hair.

'Of *working* in the press,' she says pointedly. She glances down at her clipboard. Her super-long, immaculately curled lashes flutter over her doll-face cheeks.

I hastily rub a finger beneath my eyes, suddenly aware that my mascara will have smudged me into a panda-face by now. My hair isn't the only thing that tends to have gone nuts by home-time.

'Wow! Which paper does your father work for?' one of the twins pipes up.

Cindy appears to blush, but I decide it must be a trick of the light in the dingy room.

'Is it one of the broadsheets?' the other twin asks excitedly.

'*The-Green-Park-Advertiser*,' Cindy mutters so quickly it seems like one word.

'The what?' Will immediately asks with a smirk.

'*The Green Park Advertiser*,' Cindy repeats and now I can see for sure that her cheeks are aflame. 'But anyway, that's beside the point,' she continues. 'The webzine will be sent to every student's school email address as an attachment each Wednesday. This means I'll need your articles handed in promptly on Monday to give me a chance to read them and make any rewrites I think necessary. We'll have an editorial meeting every Monday after school for you to hand in your articles, but this room will be open for us to use during the week too.'

Will's head jerks up. 'Do we get a final say on your rewrites? I've won prizes for my writing. I don't think I'm going to be needing your *help*.' He says 'help' like he's spitting out a slug. Wow. Doll-faces mean nothing to this boy. Unless the sparks I feel shooting between him and Cindy are sparks of passion.

*No.*

I trash the thought. Will is obviously the sort of boy who ruffles Cindy's feathers and, looking at her sleek'n'shiny shoulder-length hair, I decide 'ruffled' is probably not Cindy's style.

'Of course I'll give you a chance to provide your input,' Cindy says to Will. 'But *I'll* be pressing the Send button, so *I'll* have the final say.'

Will opens his mouth to argue, but Mr Harris butts in. 'I know you're a very accomplished writer, Will, but even the best writers need an editor. Let's just see how it goes, eh?' he suggests soothingly.

Cindy continues. 'We'll also have our own page on the school website so we can get feedback directly from our readers.'

'Cool,' Sam says, nodding.

'I want this webzine to be read by every student at Green Park.' Cindy unhooks a wad of paper from her clipboard and starts handing out sheets to each of us. 'I want publication day to be a day the whole school looks forward to.'

I take a sheet and look at it.

*Green Park High Webzine Mission Statement.*

Will groans.

'Thank you, Will.' Cindy gives the last sheet to Mr Harris. 'Your thoughts will be welcome, once we've read through the text.'

'Yes, Miss Jensen,' Will says with a smirk.

Barbara's unzipping her pencil case and rooting for a pen. 'I think it's a good idea to get our goals sorted out before we begin,' she says, unsurprisingly backing up Cindy.

Jeff sniffs. 'The only goals I'm interested in are on the pitch.'

Cindy rolls her eyes at Mr Harris. 'Any tips on how to engage the boys, Mr Harris?'

'You're doing wonderfully,' Mr Harris tells her.

Personally, I'm on the boys' side. This is a school webzine, not a global corporation. But I don't comment. If this is what it takes to get every student reading my articles then I'm OK with it.

'Now,' Cindy begins, 'my father says all the best publications are guided by a comprehensive mission statement. I don't see why our webzine should be any different.' She starts to read from her sheet. 'Point one: the Green Park webzine aims to be the best friend today's teen is searching for.'

'Oh, yes.' Barbara's nodding. 'We must be a voice our fellow students want to listen to.'

'Exactly,' Cindy agrees.

Will rolls the corner of his sheet between his finger and thumb. 'How long have you two been rehearsing this?'

Barbara blushes bright red. 'We haven't.'

Cindy gives Will a look that would wither a cactus. 'Barbie and I have been friends for a gazillion years. Is it really so surprising we're on the same page mentally?'

Jeff rubs his nose. '*Mentally* is right.'

Sam chuckles. 'Give her a break.' He flicks his sheet. 'She has got eleven more points to get through.'

'Yes, well.' Cindy clears her throat. She looks like she never expected this to be so difficult. 'Let's skip to the last point, which is the most important one. You can read the rest yourselves later.' She scans through the words, pausing at the bottom of the page, 'Point twelve:

our webzine seeks to enhance the wonderful sense of community already enjoyed by the students of Green Park High.'

'More enjoyment.' Sam folds the paper in four and stuffs it in his pocket. 'I'll go for that.'

'Exactly, Sam.' Cindy tugs another piece of paper from her clipboard. 'Above all, I hope we can have some fun with this project.'

'And share that fun with our readers.' Barbara sounds excited.

I *feel* excited. Even with Cindy's naff mission statement, this webzine is going to be great. I can't wait to get started. Once I've saved the bike shed, I can move on to longer lunch breaks, shorter lessons, unlimited Wi-Fi on school grounds . . .

Cindy interrupts my train of thought. 'Thank you to those of you who emailed you'd be coming today. It's given me the chance to assign each of you a role.' She picks up another wad of paper from the desk. 'I've typed you each a set of guidelines to help you.'

I sit up straight. I never emailed. What will my assignment be?

She turns to Sam. He's practising guitar chords in the air. Cindy smiles at him patiently and he looks up, clearly surprised by the sudden quiet.

'Sam, I'd love for you to be our music reporter,' Cindy says. 'Since you're in a band.'

'Great. Thanks.' Sam nods and goes back to air-guitaring.

'I'm giving you complete freedom to choose the bands you want to report on.' She sounds a bit breathless. 'I want your column to reflect your tastes and your thoughts.' Her voice is soft and gooey. Is the Ice Queen *melting*? I suddenly picture her sitting on a perfectly pink bed in a perfectly pink bedroom, popping strawberry creams from a chocolate box and writing long love letters in exquisite handwriting. Could the Ice Queen have a marshmallow heart? Now *that* would make a great article – *Jensen's Soft Centre Revealed: In-depth Exposé*.

Sam's screwing up his face as though he's trying to reach a particularly difficult chord.

'Sam?' Cindy prompts.

'Complete freedom, my tastes, my thoughts,' Sam parrots before taking his guidelines from her.

Cindy's lips tighten and she turns to Will. 'You'll be our senior news reporter,' she tells him.

'OK,' Will looks grudgingly satisfied as he takes his handout.

'Phillip and David, I know you expressed an interest in technology in your email to me, so I've decided that you can be the gadget and software reviewers.' Cindy hands the twins their own guidelines, which they immediately start to study eagerly.

'And Jeff.' Cindy taps her clipboard decisively with her pen. 'You'll be the sports reporter.'

Jeff looks over at Mr Harris. 'Really?'

Mr Harris nods and Jeff's face breaks into a grin. I file away my first mental note for Treacle – *eyes sparkle when he smiles*.

'That's great.' Jeff picks up his sports bag from the floor. 'Is it all right if I head off now? I'm late for football practice.'

'Just one more thing.' Cindy hands him his sheet of paper and clears her throat. 'I'll need a report on *all* the week's matches – football, netball, hockey, whatever. Do you think you can manage that?'

'Even the *girls'* teams?' Jeff raises his eyebrows.

'Well, duh!' Cindy tucks a hair behind her ear. 'Half our readership will be girls.'

*Excellent!* This is even better than I could have planned. Jeff will have to watch Treacle in action on the pitch. Hopefully, once he's seen her play, he'll be blown away. I imagine him standing on the goal line, stunned by her skill as she lands one in the back of the net. I picture him cheering, his eyes glowing with admiration. '*Oh, Treacle, you were brilliant!*' he cries, catching her in his arms as she runs off the pitch and swinging her round. '*I don't know how I never saw it before.*'

Back in the real world, the door swings shut behind Jeff as he leaves for practice and Cindy turns her attention to Barbara. Barbara blinks up at her eagerly.

She reminds me of a doting puppy waiting to be thrown a treat.

'Barbie, you'll be lifestyle features writer,' Cindy tells her. 'I'll need five hundred words a week on something that's important to the students at Green Park High.'

'Yes, Cindy.' Barbara scribbles a note in her jotter before taking her handout.

Now *I'm* blinking at Cindy like a puppy. She's giving out *great* assignments. What will mine be? Even if I didn't email her, there must be something left. Current affairs reporter? Student news editor? My palms itch. I want to blurt out my plan for the bike shed piece, but my tongue is welded to the roof of my mouth. How can *I*, a lowly Year Nine, tell these Year Tens my idea? What if they think it sucks?

Cindy doesn't even look at me. 'I'll be writing the weekly beauty and fashion column,' she announces. 'I want to make sure that our first edition is really great, so I think we should have an extra meeting this week too, now that everyone has their assignments. We'll meet here tomorrow at one.'

Will gets to his feet and heaves his backpack on to his shoulder. 'Fine, I'll tell Jeff about the extra meeting,' he says, making his way to the door.

Sam drops his air guitar. 'Are we finished?'

Cindy makes a final tick on her clipboard and then flashes him a smile that would burn through fog. 'Yes. See you tomorrow.'

Sam nods and grins at me as he walks past and out of the room. The twins follow him, chattering excitedly about which computer game they will review first.

Mr Harris tries to button his jacket, but can't find a button, just the empty threads where buttons used to be. 'Nicely done,' he praises Cindy and heads for the door.

'I need to get some books from my locker, Cindy,' Barbara calls, pushing her glasses up her nose. 'I'll meet you at the gate.'

'Great.' Cindy is zipping her clipboard into her bag as Barbara and Mr Harris exit the storeroom.

*It's over?*

*Is that it?*

I feel stunned. 'What about me, Cindy?' My question comes out in a squeak. I swallow and summon all my courage then say louder, 'What's *my* assignment?'

Cindy looks at me blankly, as if she'd forgotten I was even there. Probably because she had. After a few seconds' silence, she starts to smile. But her eyes remain cool. 'Ah, yes, Gemma, is it? I have just the thing for you.'

I hold my breath. This is it. My first writing assignment. In my head I'm holding up that award again '. . . *thank you, Spellcheck, thank you, Google . . .*'

Cindy's smile now seems more of a smirk. 'It's something no good webzine can be without. I'm sure that you'll be perfect for it . . .'

'The horoscopes?' Treacle falls back on the sofa, belly-laughing so loud that Mum shouts down the stairs.

'Cut the cackle, girls! I'm trying to get Ben to bed!'

'Sorry, Mum.' I swing the living room door shut with my foot and smother Treacle's squawks with a cushion. My brother Ben has cystic fibrosis so he needs a good night's sleep to keep his strength up.

Treacle fights me off and sits up. 'Nice career move, Mystic Mug.'

I flop down on the rug and hug the cushion. 'Cindy said I'd be perfect for the column.'

'Why? Does she think all Year Nines are psychic?' Treacle rolls her eyes. 'What did she say when you turned her down?'

'Nothing.'

'Nothing?'

I stare at the floor. 'I didn't turn her down.'

'What?' Treacle shrieks.

'Shh.'

'You said *yes*?'

26

I shrug. 'I know it's not what I'd hoped for but—'

'The *horoscopes*?' Treacle cuts in. 'Do they hand out Nobel prizes for horoscopy?'

'Astrology,' I correct.

'Whatever.'

'It's not like I had a choice. Being the only Year Nine in a pack of Year Tens is a bit like being Baby Bear in a room full of Goldilocks. They're sharing out the porridge while I'm wondering who broke my chair.'

Treacle leans back into the sofa. 'Don't worry.' She grins. 'Baby Bears eventually grow into Grizzlies. At least you got a job, and I'm sure it will lead on to something better. Maybe next term she'll let you do the problem page.'

'Oh, ha ha.' We look at each other and start to laugh.

Then Treacle's smile wavers. 'I saw Jeff at football practice today.'

She's looking wistful. I could cheer her up right now by telling her Jeff is working on the webzine – which is practically a backstage pass to his life. But I'm saving the news for a maximum-impact headline. Besides, I have to let her dangle a bit longer while I follow my journalistic instinct and check the facts. 'Did he see you? Did you say hi?'

'Why would I say *hi*?' Treacle's open-mouthed. 'He doesn't know I'm alive.'

'But you gave him his ball back in the playground this morning.'

'That doesn't mean I can *Hi* him whenever I like!' Treacle lobs a cushion at me. 'Don't be dumb.'

'But if you never *Hi* him, he'll never *Hi* you back.'

'But what if he blanks me?' she says, looking worried.

'Jeff wouldn't do that.'

'How do *you* know?'

I smile. I've got her complete attention. It's the perfect time to drop my info-bomb. 'He's working on the webzine,' I say casually.

'*What?*' She's hanging off the front of the sofa like a chimp begging for a banana. '*Writing?*'

'Some kind of extra credit thing with Mr Harris.' I shrug. I'm still acting cool but I'm savouring the moment. 'He's going to be the sports writer.'

If Treacle were a cartoon character, her eyes would be spinning and zigzags would be shooting from her head. 'You're going to be working with Jeff? Why didn't you tell me?'

'I'm telling you now.'

Treacle throws up her arms like she's high-fiving angels. Then she stops and droops. 'This is so unfair! You're going to get to work with him, but what about me? How am I ever going to get him to see me as a *girl* and not just something that kicks a ball about?'

I look at Treacle. With her baggy joggers, shapeless football jersey and hair skewed in a ponytail, even *I'm* having trouble seeing her as a girl.

'Perhaps if you dressed more …' I fumble for the right word, feeling guilty for even thinking it, '… *girly?*'

'But I'm comfortable like this.' Treacle looks fondly down at her outfit. 'It's my number ten shirt. I always score when I'm wearing my number ten shirt.'

'Yes, but are you going to score with a *boy* when you're wearing it?' I point out.

Her eyes pop. 'You want me to dress like Savannah, don't you? I'd *never* carry it off.'

'Why not?'

'You know Savannah! She's cooler than an Eskimo eating an ice lolly in a snowdrift. Coolness is part of her operating system.' Treacle shrugs. 'If I wore a skirt as short as hers, my knees would start shouting, "Look at us! We're the knobbly twins!"'

'Your knees aren't knobbly!' Treacle's got great knees – though admittedly, I've only ever seen them splattered with mud on a football pitch.

'They're like oversized walnuts!' she argues. 'Where is Savannah, anyway? She said she'd be here at seven.'

'Probably still deciding who to date,' I say with a laugh. Suddenly I have an idea. 'There's an article in *Teengirl* about how to get noticed by boys.' I pull Treacle to her feet and shunt her towards the door. 'It's in my room.'

'There's *always* an article in *Teengirl* about how to get

noticed by boys,' Treacle sniffs, trudging after me as I bound upstairs.

As we reach the top and head along the hall, I can hear Mum bargaining with Ben in his room.

'If you go to bed now, you can get up early and play on your Xbox.'

'But Mum, why can't I play Xbox now and sleep late in the morning?'

We creep past his door and slip into my bedroom.

'This article's different.' I scoop the mag off my desk and show it to Treacle.

'Oh, great.' She snatches it off me and flops on to my bed. '*Ten Ways to Nab Your Lad*. Well, I need about a hundred!'

I ignore her whinging and rummage through my wardrobe. What Treacle needs is tough love not sympathy. 'Here.' I toss a chocolate-coloured miniskirt at her, and a turquoise top Dad says I'll freeze to death in, which must mean it's gorgeous.

'Right.' I use my fierce voice. I've got to get Treacle out of her football jersey. 'You change into those and then come downstairs so we can practise The Walk.'

'The *Walk*?' Treacle sounds horrified, but before she can moan any more I leave her to get changed and take the magazine downstairs. There's a whole paragraph on walking in the article. By the time I've finished she's going to be strutting like a supermodel.

I'm so busy skim-reading, I don't notice Ben's shoes parked at the bottom of the stairs. I stumble over them and find myself hurtling into the living room a lot faster than I'd intended.

I grab for the sofa and collapse into it. *Teengirl* slaps on to the cushion beside me, flopping open on the horoscope page.

The shiny words shout at me: *What do the stars say about your life, love and luck?*

I wince, remembering my super-uncool assignment for the webzine, and flick the living door closed with an outstretched toe.

*Libra.* I'm trying not to read it but I can't tear my gaze away.

*This week, take care of yourself! Manicures and pedicures, a relaxing face mask, and a good night's sleep are all part of the plan. Swathe yourself in satin and lace and indulge in every girl's fashion dream.*

Oh, please. It's so lame.

Is this going to be my life? A hack journalist churning out fluff pieces for a hard-faced editor.

A Despair Monster starts tap-dancing on my chest, delighted at recruiting a new member to its dark world of endless misery. I picture my awards ceremony. It's not me on the podium any more. A glamorous blonde with perfectly straight hair is holding up the award while the audience cheer. I'm sitting at the back, slow-clapping next to a weather girl from breakfast TV.

Weather girl leans closer. 'Did you say you wrote horoscopes?'

I sigh. 'Yes.'

'Do you know what's in store for Capricorn this week?' She smiles a glittering smile, utterly unaware that no one ever asks me anything else any more.

As I reach for a napkin and prepare to gag her, the living room door eases open and Treacle slides in. Jerked back to reality, I sit up.

Her knees are pressed together like she's trying to hide them both at the same time.

'You look great!' Weather girl puffs out of existence and I focus on Treacle. She looks fab. The turquoise top and chocolate skirt are gorgeous on her. All her football training has toned her into a complete babe. I just wish *she* knew it. Right now, she's fidgeting like the outfit's wearing her, not the other way round.

As Treacle shuffles further into the room, the doorbell rings.

Mum calls from the hall. 'Savannah's here!'

I sit bolt upright. 'Treacle, don't tell her about the horoscopes!'

'Why not?'

'Not my proudest moment.'

'OK.'

'You swear?'

'I swear.' Treacle nods.

'On your mum's Jimmy Choos?'

'On my mum's *what*?'

'Did someone say Jimmy Choos?' Savannah whisks in and drapes herself across an armchair, long legs swinging over the edge, arms drooping, hair cascading round her face.

'Jim he chews? Chews what?' Treacle's sitting, eyebrows and palms raised like we're speaking Martian.

Savannah shakes her head sadly. 'Shoes, Treacle. They're shoes.' She glances down at Treacle's trainers. '*Real* shoes.'

'Like Nikes but with heels and slingbacks and stuff,' I explain. I'm no expert at fashion, but occasionally, when Savannah squeals and waves this month's copy of *Elle* in my face, I look and learn. I figure if you're going to be a journalist, you've got to know what's happening in every walk of life – including the catwalk.

Treacle slumps back in the sofa. 'I'm never going to understand this girly stuff.'

Savannah looks at Treacle properly and stares at her, mouth wide. She's probably never seen Treacle in a skirt before. 'Nice legs, Treacle.' She nods approvingly. 'You should show them off more often. In fact,' she sits up, 'if you want to get Jeff's attention, you should try wearing that outfit on the pitch. You look great.'

Treacle snorts. 'Not exactly practical for tackling.'

'Right, let's get back to the article,' I say, flicking to the right page. 'We're taking some tips from *Teengirl*,' I explain to Savannah.

Savannah raises a perfectly plucked eyebrow. 'Tips on what?'

'How to get a boy,' I reply.

'What for?' Savannah exclaims, with all the shock of someone who has never needed a tip on getting a boy in her entire life.

Treacle's face flushes redder than a stop sign.

'Just for fun,' I say quickly. I don't want Treacle giving up out of embarrassment before we've even started.

'Oh. Cool!' Savannah says.

I throw Treacle an encouraging smile. '*You're a girl with more than attitude – you've got sass-itude!*' I start reading from the glossy pink page. '*Don't wilt like a daisy at sundown. Think sunflower! Stand tall!*'

Treacle grimaces and straightens up.

'*Stand with your hips pulled back and your backbone straight.*'

'You look like you've got wind,' Savannah snorts.

Ignoring her, I press on. '*Chin out and eyes facing front.*'

Treacle thrusts out her chin and glares like Mrs Monroe, our super-scary maths teacher. She looks like she's about to shred anyone in her path and throw the scraps out of the window. Once again Savannah starts to laugh.

34

'Any chance you can drop the psycho-killer expression?' I ask sweetly.

'Try pouting like a supermodel,' Savannah suggests.

Treacle cuts the glare, then goggles her eyes and lets her mouth droop into a *Vogue* pout. 'Is that better?'

'You look less scary,' I say helpfully, realising suddenly that the line between goddess and freak is very thin. Right now, Treacle is wobbling towards freak and I'm trying hard not to giggle.

'This is so funny!' Savannah cries, clapping her hands together. 'Read some more!'

I focus on the mag and carry on. '*Your hair may shine, your eyes may sparkle, but your walk will give away what's on the* inside, *so don't shuffle, strut!*' Who writes this stuff? '*Be comfortable. Wear shoes you can balance in. Falling over is not an option if you're trying to make a good impression.*'

'Ha – no danger there,' Savannah says, looking at Treacle's feet. I follow her gaze. Treacle's still wearing her trainers. She looks like a gazelle in wellies.

I don't comment. We can move on to footwear later. 'Start walking,' I tell her, reading from the article again. '*Don't stride. Let the air waft you forward. Float like dandelion seed. Let your arms swing freely. There's no need to pump them. You're not in the gym.*'

Treacle starts striding across the carpet, chin forward, bum out, arms swaying like they've got no bones. She looks more like a chimp in the zoo than a model on the catwalk.

'Don't lean forward, lean back!' I order. *'Lead with your hips.'*

She fires her hips forward, her head snapping back.

'Oh, Treacle, you're hilarious!' Savannah exclaims. Treacle glares at her.

'What? I thought you were joking,' Savannah says.

'Let's try the other stuff they recommend,' I say quickly and carry on reading out loud. *'Try "sweetening up" your behaviour: why laugh when you can giggle? Why tease when you can compliment? Come on, girls! Don't just smoothe off your rough edges, add some pink frills to them.'* I can feel waves of disbelief rolling off Treacle but I don't stop. *'Don't shake someone's hand – kiss their cheek and, if you leave a lipstick print, all the better! Just apologise prettily and dab it off with your hanky. Be cute. Smile more often and speak in a higher-pitched voice.'*

'OK, Gemmakins,' Treacle squeaks. She's standing on tiptoe, a grotesque ballerina, batting her eyelashes like a camel trying to get sand out of its eye.

Savannah lets out a roar of laughter and even I can't hold it in any longer. I explode into giggles, dropping *Teengirl* on to the floor. Thankfully Treacle bursts into laughter too and we all fall back on the sofa, hooting helplessly.

'I really don't think—' Treacle's gasping for breath, '—

Jeff's going to be rushing for a date if he sees me like that.'

I'm fighting hiccups. 'No,' I splutter. 'Maybe we need to try a different approach.'

'Yes, one where I don't look like I need the loo,' Treacle replies.

'You just need to be yourself,' Savannah says, flicking her glossy hair over her shoulder. 'You want a boy to like you for who you are, not someone you're pretending to be.'

'Savannah's right.' I start to smile. 'And I've got some great news.'

Treacle looks up like a spaniel who's heard the word *walkies*.

'Since Jeff's working on the webzine . . .' I begin.

Treacle's bolt upright now. 'Yeah?'

'He'll be watching *all* of the school matches.'

Treacle's flushing. 'OMG!' she gasps. 'Even the girls'?'

'Uh-huh.' I'm smiling. 'And while you're busy impressing him on the field, I'll be finding out everything I can about him in our meetings.'

'Good work!' Savannah says approvingly.

Treacle starts flapping her hands like she's drying nail varnish. 'You can find out if he's noticed me.'

I nod. 'And what he likes and doesn't like.' I'm so happy she's smiling. 'I'll make a note of everything and report back.'

'Nice plan.' Savannah looks at her watch. 'Right, I've got to go.'

'Already?' Treacle and I chorus.

Savannah stands up and smoothes her skirt, not that there's much of it to smoothe. But with legs like Savannah's who needs a skirt? 'Fraid so, I'm meeting Josh at eight. Poor Marcus was crushed. But I couldn't *two-time*.'

'Where's Josh taking you?' I ask.

'*I'm* taking *him* to the movies,' Savannah says, heading for the door. 'Some shoot-'em-up action thingy. It's always best to make a fuss of them on the first date. He'll be so grateful, I'll get to pick the next five dates.'

I'm confused. 'But you picked this one.'

'Yes, but I picked it for *him*. The next ones I'll pick for me.' She sweeps out and the front door clicks shut behind her.

'Was she born knowing this stuff?' Treacle says, staring after her.

I grin. 'Perhaps she gets it from magazines.' We both look at *Teengirl* lying on the rug where I dropped it.

'Talking of which.' Treacle's gaze zooms in on me. 'When's your first load of *horror*-scopes due?'

'Monday.'

Treacle leans forward. Her ponytail swings as she tips her head. 'So you're really OK with doing them?'

'It's a start.' I'm determined to look on the bright side. 'And at least I'll finally have my name in print.'

# 4

'Ow, not so hard!'

Ben shouts at me and starts coughing. He's lying on his nearly-new, super-cool, bells-and-whistles tilt-table, fully adjustable to 1001 positions. Right now he's on his back, stretched flat, sloping head first towards the floor while I pound his chest like he's a pair of bongos. Doing this for twenty minutes each morning is part of his treatment; it helps to clear his lungs. 'Do you want to sing today?'

'No.'

Ben's in a growly mood. I'm not surprised. His CF is hard work. He's only nine years old and all the pills and inhalers and therapy and exercise are Not Fun. Plus they seriously cut into his Xbox time. He can't do sleepovers either or scoff down pizza without taking a fistful of pills to help him digest it.

Singing sometimes helps take his mind off the physio. I start warbling, hoping he'll join in. On a good day, the daft wobble that I thump into his voice makes him laugh. But today he doesn't want to play.

I stop yodelling and try patting out rhythms on his chest, hoping it'll feel more like fun for both of us.

I've been taking turns with Mum and Dad to help with his physio for as long as I can remember. I like helping out, but it's hard work. When I'm a famous journalist, the first thing I'm going to buy him is a vibrating air vest. After that, I'm going to pay for him to visit a specialist clinic in Sweden where they've got some pretty amazing therapies.

I drift a little, still pummelling his chest, while in my head I'm taking interviews after my awards ceremony.

'I only hope that now I can make my family's life a little easier,' I tell *The Times*' media correspondent. In my imagination, he's really handsome and terribly impressed by my brilliance.

'Has your brother's illness been important in driving you on to such great success?' he asks sympathetically.

I touch his knee and look at him earnestly. 'My pure love of journalism is what's driven me,' I admit. 'But Ben's illness has taught me a lot about loyalty and tenacity. And about facing the truth head-on.'

As his eyes glow in admiration, Mum shouts from the bathroom. 'Has Ben taken his vitamins and antibiotics?' I'm jolted from my fantasy.

'Not yet, but I've got them ready.' I've already lined up the pill bottles on the table. Mum asks the same question every time it's my turn to do Ben's therapy, like I might *forget*. It used to bug me till I realised she needs to ask; it's her magic spell that keeps Ben from getting an infection. If she asks then he'll be OK for the day. Like if I check under my bed for alligators before I switch off the light, there'll be no alligator. It sounds crazy, I know, but I haven't been bitten by an alligator yet.

The morning passes slowly. Maths drags like time's trailing through syrup. I'm relieved when the lunch bell goes. My physio mornings with Ben always make me tired. I have to set the alarm early and then run for the bus.

'Is my hair OK?' I ask as I head for the lunch hall with Treacle and Savannah.

'Try this.' Treacle stops and slides a hairband from her wrist.

Facing the class with hedge-hair is one thing; facing a packed lunch hall is entirely different.

Ducking behind me, she scoops my hair loosely into a low ponytail. 'I wish I had curly hair like yours.'

I stare at her silky black locks. 'We should swap.' We've been longing to swap hair since nursery school, but we haven't discovered how to do a whole-head hair transplant yet. If we ever do, I bet she lasts five minutes before she's begging me to swap back. My hair is not exactly wash-and-go. It's more light-the-fuse-and-retreat.

'Wait a second.' Savannah pulls a few stray tendrils

round my face. 'That's better,' she says, standing back and admiring her handiwork. 'Très chic!'

The lunch hall is warm, wide and sunny. Students mill at the edges and fill the Formica tables. We take a seat at the table by the pasta bar and I scope the hall, self-conscious as I recognise Cindy, Barbara, Sam, Will and Jeff, dotted around the room. I wonder if I'm allowed to say hi to them. We work together on the webzine, but does that mean I can speak to them outside our meetings? I freeze as I catch Sam's eye. Shyness swamps me and I look away, feeling dumb. Savannah would have just flashed a smile and got on with her lunch. For the millionth time I wish I was her. I fumble with my sandwich box, the sting of a blush heating my face.

Savannah's phone bleeps and she checks the screen. 'Text from Josh,' she says casually, as if getting a text from a boy is as dull and everyday as cleaning your teeth.

'Aren't you going to read it?' I ask.

Savannah unwraps a ham-and-lettuce sandwich, cut into four neat little triangles – even her lunch is poster-perfect. 'When I'm ready,' she says with a grin. 'Don't want him thinking I'm too keen.'

'I've gotta eat fast,' Treacle says. 'It's the Cup match tomorrow and I want to practise penalties.' Her feet are tapping under her chair. I know she's itching to get to the football field.

She gobbles her sandwich, stuffing crisps between each mouthful of tuna-filled bread.

I nibble the samosa Mum packed for my lunch and keep my eyes fixed firmly on Treacle or my lunch box. There's no way I'm letting my gaze stray towards the webziners again. But as always I can't keep my mind from wandering.

### Girl Dies of Embarrassment in Lunch Hall.

*A teenage girl shrivelled up and collapsed into her lunch box yesterday after she was spotted looking at a boy in the year above her. The reckless student lost control of her eyeballs and found herself staring into a crowd of older students. Before she had a chance to look away, she was caught and immediately zapped by the God of Embarrassment before she could break any more school taboos.*

*'It was a blessing she died quickly,' her friend Treacle was quoted as saying. 'It would have been worse if she'd lived – the humiliation would have followed her through the rest of her school life.'*

Treacle's voice cuts into my think-piece. 'Right, I'm off,' she says as she scrunches up her crisp packet.

I drop the half-eaten samosa back into my lunch box, my appetite crushed by my drama-queen daydream.

Treacle doesn't notice. 'If I score ten penalties before the bell goes,' she says, 'we'll win the Cup.'

She's making deals just like Mum does with Ben and I do with alligators. Maybe everyone needs magical deals to make them feel strong. No wonder Cindy wants horoscopes in the school webzine. Half the school may have smartphones, but we're still as superstitious as cave-dwellers. 'You'll win,' I promise.

'Thanks. See you in geography.' Treacle clatters her chair back and makes for the exit. She's already wearing her number ten football jersey over her school jumper.

I close my lunch box. I might as well leave too. I'm not hungry and Savannah is now deep in conversation with Sally Moore about the pros and cons of carbs. 'See you in geography,' I call to them.

'Yeah.' Savannah waves at me, distracted.

I hop to my feet and zigzag between the tables. I slide past Will. He's tipping back in his chair, feet on table, hands behind head. Sam's sitting next to him, blond hair crowding his eyes, leaning forward, hands waving as he talks to Will. I sneek a peek, careful not to make eye contact this time. From the intense look on Sam's face he must be critiquing a new album or explaining a new riff. Will's scanning the room, his gaze at knee height. Checking out this season's shorter skirt length?

He's *really is* gawping, his chair creaking as Sally leans across her table to reach the salt. I pause behind him. 'Cindy should've made you fashion correspondent,' I mutter.

44

I didn't mean to be heard, but a lull in the lunch hall hubbub leaves a hole of silence, which my comment fills like a bell in a cathedral. I freeze in horror as Will turns and stares at me.

'What?'

'N-n-nothing,' I stammer, face on fire.

Sam laughs, his blue eyes flashing at me. Mortified, I push through a bunch of kids and head out the door.

The corridors are empty. Anyone not in the dining room is at the shops or behind the bike shed. I take a few deep breaths, letting my blush cool as I head for the webzine storeroom.

### Year Nine Shot at Dawn

*Gemma Stone was executed today after being found guilty of repeatedly harassing Year Tens. After a gawking incident earlier in the day, the idiot Year Nine actually dared to speak to one of the coolest Year Tens in the country, even though she'd not been spoken to first.*

*Authorities announced the death sentence shortly after lunch. 'We need to ensure that Year Tens feel safe from such barefaced cheek. Stone's execution should serve as a warning to any other Year Nines foolish enough to cross the Unspoken Divide.'*

I blank out the Lunch Hall Fiasco before the headlines flashing through my head kill me. Instead, I focus on my column. *Horoscopes*. I shudder. A night's sleep hasn't made the idea any more appealing.

I sigh as I mount the stairs. Now I'm lumbered with the horoscopes I guess my Save Our Shed campaign is dead in the water.

The door of the storeroom's ajar. I swing it open, amazed at the transformation. The tangled heaps of chairs and tottering book stacks have disappeared. Four desks are arranged neatly, each with a computer humming on top. Cindy's sitting at one, the glare from the screen making her perfect skin glow.

'Hi, Gemma.' She's scribbling notes on a piece of paper beside her keyboard. 'I'm glad to see someone's made an effort to get here on time.'

'I-I . . .' I'm still staring at the room. It actually looks more like an office than a storeroom now. 'What happened in here?'

'I asked the caretaker to take some of the books and unwanted furniture down to the basement.'

'And he *did*?' The caretaker's not famous for his love of work. Or kids.

'Why wouldn't he?' Cindy looks up, blue eyes wide. 'That's his job.'

'And who set these up?' I wave my hand towards the PCs.

'The twins, bless them.'

'Phil and David?'

Cindy twirls her pen in her fingers. 'They came in early this morning to give me a hand.'

Doesn't *anyone* say no to this girl? 'Which one's mine?'

Cindy shrugs. 'We're going to have to share since there's only four, so take whichever one you want.'

I head for the nearest desk. 'I'm glad you got here first.' Cindy beckons to me with her Bic. 'I need a quiet word.'

I dump my bag and go to her desk.

She waves me closer, lowering her voice so I have to lean in. 'This horoscope thing.' She keeps one eye on the door. 'I've been thinking about it and I've decided that it would be best if you write it under a pen-name.'

'A pen-name?' I jerk back and stare at her. 'Not my *own* name?'

Cindy lets out a tinkling laugh. 'Don't be silly.' She shakes her head. 'Who will believe the predictions of Gemma Stone?'

It's hard to argue. I can't even predict whether there's an alligator under my bed.

Cindy glances at the notes she's scribbled then starts typing on her keyboard. 'We need our readers to believe we have a real astrologer working on the webzine.' Her eyes are fixed on her screen.

'I guess.' I start to back away.

'So don't tell anyone. Not even the rest of the webzine team.'

'OK.' As I turn, I stumble against a desk and have to grab the monitor to stop it falling. Just as I find my feet, boys' voices echo in the corridor outside.

Cindy snaps to attention, smoothing her hair, as Sam and Will shamble into the room. Will shoots me a look that tells me he's not forgotten my lunch hall comment. He heads straight for the desk I'd chosen, picks up my bag and tosses it at me.

'I'll take this PC,' Will announces, sitting down. 'It's the newest one.'

Fury floods me, totally extinguishing the smouldering embers of my embarrassment. First Cindy casually tells me I'm not going to get my name in print. Now Will's bossing me about too.

'Here, Gemma. Use this PC.' Sam leans over the desk beside Will's and pushes the On button. His smile is interrupted by Cindy clearing her throat.

'Have you seen Phil and David?' she asks. 'They should be here by now.' She glances at the clock over the door. 'And Barbara.'

'Sorry I'm late, Cind!' Barbara barrels through the doorway. She's clutching a pile of files against her chest. Clumps of hair have escaped her bunches and are sticking out like head handles. Her skirt is twisted, rucked up at one side. She glances, blushing, at the boys, and drops the files on Cindy's desk then pulls at her skirt with one hand and pats her hair down with the other.

I slide behind a desk, quietly claiming the PC Sam started for me before anyone else arrives. I'm just in time. The nerd twins, Phil and David, pad into the room, looking like their mother dressed them. Actually, they look like Barbara's mother dressed them.

Then Jeff skids in. He's flapping a piece of paper. 'I've got this term's sports fixtures from the school office.'

'Well done.' Cindy nods approvingly.

Jeff's frowning. 'How am I meant to get to all these games?'

Cindy doesn't blink. 'Gemma can help.'

I stare at her. 'I don't know anything about sport.'

Cindy barely looks my way. 'Gemma's going to be the webzine's editorial assistant,' she announces to the room. 'So if any of you need help, she's your go-to girl.'

*I am?* What is Cindy thinking? I guess she's trying to disguise my undercover horoscopic activities. But why would anyone here come to me for help? It's like they believe their extra year of hormones has developed them into super-beings; I'm practically Neanderthal by comparison. I guess they might have some stapling they need doing. Maybe Barbara will want me to carry some of her files. I try to imagine Will asking me to help on his feature article.

In my head, he holds out his article hopefully. 'Gemma, can you proofread this?'

'Sure, Will,' I tell him.

'And if you've got any ideas, I'd appreciate hearing them,' he begs. 'I think it needs a stronger finish.'

'I'll give it some thought.' As I cast an imaginary eye over his imaginary article, reality butts in.

'Can you drop this at the office on your way back to class, Gemma?' Cindy's holding out a hole-punch. 'I promised Mrs Flint I'd get it back to her before the end of the day.'

Sam intercepts it. 'I'll be passing the office,' he says. 'I'll drop it back.'

Cindy gives him a grateful smile. 'Sam, you're a knight in shining armour.' Then she sweeps the room with a glance. 'Anybody else need Gemma to help them?' she asks, offering me up like I'm a plate of sandwiches.

Will looks me up and down as if he'd asked for a sports car and got an exercise bike.

Phil scratches his ear. 'We won't need help.'

*What a surprise.*

'But thanks, Gemma,' David adds.

*At least they're polite about it.*

'Yes,' Barbara gushes. 'Thanks, Gemma. You're going to be a lifesaver, I'm sure.' She smiles at me, tucking a wilful curl behind her ear.

'I have other news.' Cindy taps her desk with her pen. 'I've managed to persuade a wonderful astrologer, Jessica Jupiter, to write horoscopes for the webzine.'

My heart plummets. My words are going to be published under the name *Jessica Jupiter*? I sound like a cartoon character.

'Who's Jessica Jupiter?' Will asks.

'She used to work on my dad's paper,' Cindy tells him.

'And now she's working on ours?' Will looks unconvinced. 'For *free*?'

'As a favour to my dad.'

'She owes him one, eh?' Will sniggers.

'She's a friend of the *family*.' If Cindy had real-actual laser eyes, she'd be deadly. She's on her feet and heading my way, a plastic bag in her hand. What now? She tips the bag and sends an avalanche of nail varnish, lipsticks, eyeliners and tester pots scattering across my desk. 'Can you help me review these, Gemma? I'm absolutely swamped setting up templates.' She should change my job title from editorial assistant to guinea pig. I pick up a pot and read the label. Wrinkle Cream. Great. I'm still dealing with spots and she wants me to worry about wrinkles. Her lashes swoop as her gaze flutters over to Sam. 'Can you help me get started on the design of the webzine, Sam?' she asks sweetly.

I feel a prickle of disappointment as Sam nods. Isn't there anyone who can resist the command of the Ice Queen?

My internal newswire's ticking out a headline:

### Ruthless Dictator Sweeps to Victory as Opposition Crumbles.

*The last man standing was felled this afternoon in a charm offensive led by heartless dictator, Cindy Jensen. Using her gamma-ray stare and deadly lashes, Jensen used a classic pincer movement to surround the rebel army and convert them into mindless cronies. Brave resistance leader, Gemma Stone, was forced into hiding as the last remnants of her Free Speech movement melted away. Gemma smuggled out this secret message: 'I'm committed to liberating my colleagues, but without support and with little ammunition, I am helpless to stop Jensen's relentless march forward.'*

As Sam and Cindy settle behind her screen and start mumbling and swapping the mouse back and forth, I sigh and open a browser window. I'd better research astrology. It may not be the best job on the webzine, but I'm determined to do it well. Jeff's staring despondently at his long list of fixtures. Will's hammering his keyboard, frowning intently at the screen. The twins are working quietly beside each other while Barbara's sucking her pen, staring at her notepad.

'I just can't decide on this week's feature,' she sighs. 'So many things to choose from.'

Cindy glances up. 'Choose whatever's most important to you,' she suggests. 'It'll give the piece heart.'

My newswire's still ticking. What about *Cindy Jensen: My Life in Her Shadow* by Barbara Dweeb?

I could write the first line.

*Cindy Jensen may have a heart of stone, but I'll always be grateful she found a place in it for me.*

I stop. I'm being unfair. Barbara may not be the coolest girl in school, but she's not an idiot. In fact, she actually seems really nice. For all I know, Cindy might be grateful *Barbara* wants to be her friend, not the other way around. Ice Queen Cindy must have some hidden warmth that makes Barbara want to hang out with her. Once again, I imagine Cindy sitting on a perfectly pink bed in a perfectly pink bedroom. This time she's swapping secrets with Barbara.

'I've always wished I had dark hair like yours, Barbie,' Cindy confesses. 'Being a blonde is such a burden. People expect me to act as perfect as I look, and yet it's so hard to be taken seriously.'

'I take you seriously,' Barbara comforts.

Cindy pats Barbara's arm, her gaze glowing with gratitude. 'I'm so lucky to have such a good friend.' Tears well in her eyes. 'If it weren't for you, Barb, I'd have no real friends at all.'

Moved by my fantasy, I resolve to be nicer. I try to forget that Cindy's stolen my dream and replaced it with an astrological nightmare.

I pick up one of the lipsticks and stare at it, pretending

to read the manufacturer and colour number on the base. Then I type Astrology in the Search box and press Return. I've got 38,700,000 results to choose from. Hurray. Fortunately, no one can see my screen. They'll think I'm researching beauty products.

I click on the first result, barely reading it. All I can see is my column, headed by the world's dumbest name: *Jessica Jupiter*. I sigh.

At least I'm not called Ursula Uranus.

'Oh, Sam!' Cindy pushes Sam's arm, giggling. 'We can't possibly use that font.'

I grit my teeth and my resolution to be nicer collapses. Cindy is totally two-faced. *We* get the Ice Queen and Sam gets the Sugar Plum Fairy.

She shuffles her chair closer and puts her hand over his on the mouse. 'What about this one?' She moves the mouse and clicks. I look back at my screen before I throw up.

*Astrology is a set of systems, traditions and beliefs founded on the notion that the relative positions of celestial bodies can explain or predict fate, personality, human affairs and other earthly matters.*

Thanks, Wikipedia. That's a big help.

Jeff sighs and rattles his long fixture list. I freeze, brain popping as an idea clangs in my head like a virus alert.

'Hey, Jeff.' I clear my throat, self-conscious. 'It's the Year Nine girls' football team Cup game tomorrow.' *Treacle's match.*

Jeff sucks air through his teeth as he glances at his fixture list. 'Yeah,' he sighs wearily.

'That would be a great first article, wouldn't it? After all, it is a *Cup* match.'

Jeff's not looking entirely convinced so I give him the hard sell. 'If you need help, I could watch it with you and take notes for your article – as the editorial assistant.'

Jeff shrugs. 'OK.'

He's not exactly punching the air with excitement, but he said OK. It's a start. He looks at Cindy. 'Can I go now? I've got footie practice.'

Will jerks up his head. 'You don't have to ask permission.' He nods towards Cindy. 'She's not armed.'

Sam laughs. 'Not yet.'

Cindy slides him a coy look. 'The only weapon I need is my smile.'

*Blargh!*

Trying not to gag, I turn back to Jeff. He's folding the fixture list. He shoves it into his back pocket and heads for the door. 'I'll see you at the match tomorrow then,' he mutters at me as he goes.

'Great!' I grin. Result! Tomorrow I can point out Treacle every time she kicks the ball.

In my mind, I'm already on the sideline, Jeff wide-eyed

beside me as he watches Treacle hammer down the wing and score a breathtaking goal from halfway down the pitch.

'Did you see that?' I bounce excitedly at Jeff's elbow, but he's speechless. Treacle's magical playing has wowed him. He's watching her as her teammates swarm round her. When the sunlight glints off her glossy hair, the admiration in his gaze melts suddenly into love . . .

Tomorrow is going to be the best day ever.

By the time the ref blows the half-time whistle, Jeff Simpson will be head over heels for Treacle.

The form room's stuffy, even though January sleet is slapping at the windows. The class is crammed for Friday morning registration. I'm perched on a table next to Treacle by the radiator. I unbutton my jacket, swamped by the heat. Miss Davis has ticked her attendance boxes and is briefing us on our class assembly.

'The History of St Valentine's Day.' As she announces the theme, Ryan Edwards, class clown, calls across the room. 'Hey, Savannah! You've had plenty of valentines, why don't you handle this one by yourself?'

Savannah's sitting beside Josh. She scowls at Ryan. 'You handle it by yourself.' She presses closer to Josh. 'I prefer to work in pairs.' She looks at me and winks.

Josh shakes his hair out of his eyes and stares Ryan down like a well-trained watchdog.

'Hey, Miss.' Chris McLaren shoots up his hand. 'Is St Valentine the one with wings and a bow and arrow?'

'That's Cupid, stupid,' Bilal Khan snorts.

'Same thing,' Chris argues. 'Some geezer trying to hook people up.'

'That's a very astute analysis, Chris.' Miss Davis tries to channel the bickering back to the topic. 'Let's think more about what St Valentine represents.'

'Love, Miss.' Sally Moore glances up from the pocket mirror in which she's checking her make-up.

'Exactly.' Miss Davis looks relieved to be on firmer ground. 'Our assembly will be focusing on the history of St Valentine's Day. How do you think we can make that interesting for the audience?'

Ryan's feet are fidgeting like he's forgotten to take his morning medication. 'We could get Savannah and Josh to give a snogging demo,' he suggests.

Savannah snaps round, eyes flaring, but Miss Davis leaps in before she can reply.

'Ryan,' she cautions, 'leave Savannah alone.' She throws a pleading look at Anila Zajmi. 'How do *you* think we might explore the history of St Valentine's day, Anila?'

Anila is every teacher's dream – she doesn't suck up, but all the teachers know she'll be there with a relevant answer when lessons start to fray. She's helped them out of so many jams, she should get a cut of their salaries. 'We can show how love has changed over the years,' Anila answers obligingly. 'How we went from arranged marriage to internet dating.'

'Great idea.' Miss Davis looks very relieved. Boosted, she tosses a follow-up question at the class. 'Where could we look if we want to find out how people thought and felt about love in the past?'

'Match.com?' Bilal calls.

'In . . . the . . . past, Bilal,' Miss Davis reiterates slowly.

'What about looking in old books?' Sally's suggestion is tentative.

Miss Davis leaps on it like a fox on a rabbit. 'Old books! Very good! Where else?'

While my classmates fling ideas at each other, I shrink into my backpack. Assemblies aren't my thing. I'm staying quiet and leaving this performance to the X Factor wannabes.

Wannabe Number One, Chelsea Leeson, is leaning against the window sill throwing poisonous eye-darts at Savannah.

I nudge Treacle. 'Is it my imagination or is Chelsea looking a little green this morning?'

Treacle scratches her nose. 'I'm not surprised, she's been wanting a slice of Joshy-pie for months.'

Savannah's too busy fluttering her eyelashes at Josh to feel Chelsea's scorching gaze. I've not had a chance to ask her, how her date went but, from the knowing way he's grinning at her I'm guessing it went well.

Poor Marcus. He's watching from the back of the class, his shoulders drooping.

'Marcus looks like someone ate his homework,' I whisper to Treacle.

She glances over her shoulder. 'Poor Marcus.'

'Yeah.' Sympathy pricks me. 'It must've taken a lot of courage to ask Savannah out.' Marcus is sweet-looking, but he's not in Josh's league. He's gazing at Savannah while Savannah gazes at Josh. Josh sniffs and inspects his fingertips, then flicks dirt out from under a nail.

Miss Davis taps her desk with her pen. The class have wandered off topic again. Sally is arguing with Bilal. 'Asking someone out via text is so *not* cool.'

Miss Davis breaks it up. 'Don't forget that St Valentine was a martyr. It might be nice to focus on the sacrifices we sometimes have to make for people we love.'

I think of Ben. And the holiday we didn't have last year because he needed a tilt-table for his physio. We could all have used a holiday. But, like Mum says, you can't have your cake and eat it.

Miss Davis raises her voice over the background chatter. 'Perhaps we could focus on some great love stories or poems,' she suggests. Her eyes are misty behind her owl-glasses. She sounds wistful. Is she single? I check out her fingers: no wedding ring. Maybe she's got a boyfriend. She could probably get one. She's not *that* old, though she'd look younger if she gave up the bun and sensible shoes. Maybe she babes it up when school's out. I try to imagine her in a tube dress and heels. Not bad. DD as Savannah would say – *Definitely Datable*.

'Do you think Miss Davis gets many valentine cards?' I whisper in Treacle's ear.

'I bet she gets more than me.' Treacle winds a long wisp of hair round her finger and sighs.

'You never know.' I smile to myself. If everything goes according to plan at the webzine, Treacle might be getting her very first card from Jeff.

'Right.' Jeff hands me a notepad and pen. 'You log the stats.'

'I *what*?' I squint at him through the freezing rain.

'Just make a note every time someone makes an attempt on goal, offsides, fouls, saves, how many corners. All the important stuff.'

I take a look at the windswept pitch. 'Well, there are four corners . . .'

'Ha ha.' Jeff shakes his head, but I wasn't joking. What does he mean, how many corners?

The teams start to file on to the pitch. Anila, from our class, is first on, followed by Karen Marsden from another Year Nine form with her mates Erin Slater and Jing-Wei Wu. Where's Treacle?

I didn't warn her Jeff was going to be watching. She was so nervous about the game. I didn't want to make it worse. But I know that, once she's on the pitch, her pre-match jitters will disappear. They always do. After that, even Jeff Simpson won't distract her from the game.

I huddle deeper into my duffle, flinching from the biting wind snapping at my cheeks. Jeff's wrapped in a scarf, his dark-blond wavy hair plastered around his face. I can see why Treacle likes him. Even half-drowned, his nose red with cold, he's DD. Not my type (although I'm not even sure I really have a type?) but Definitely Datable.

Treacle jogs on to the field and I wave. She must be freezing even though she's wearing leggings under her baggy strip. She waves back, her hand stalling in the air as she spots Jeff. I grin at her madly. She must be *so* pleased he's here.

The teams fan out into position and the ref blows his whistle.

I write *Cup Match: Green Park v Tiptonville High* on the notepad and start scanning the game for stuff to write down. There's a lot of running as the teams punt the ball around, but no one's near a goal. My gaze sneaks sideways to Jeff. Is he watching Treacle? He cups his hands round his mouth and yells encouragement to the Green Park High team.

There's a smattering of spectators, hunched against the icy wind at the edges of the pitch.

'Come on, Treacle!' I whoop.

Treacle glances at me as she thunders past, sliding to

tackle the ball away from a defender on the other team.

'Isn't she great?' I nod at Jeff.

He's watching her dribble the ball over the muddy grass as she heads towards the other team's goal. 'Yeah.' His eyes are fixed on Treacle's legs as she hammers the ball towards the net. It veers in the wind and slices past the post.

'Missed.' Jeff shakes his head.

I write, 'Goal attempt by Treacle.' My fingers are trembling and not just from cold. Jeff was really watching her! I want to jump up and down with excitement. My plan's working. *Come on, Treacle, impress him!*

Imagine if this was the beginning of something big. My pen drifts across the soggy page, drawing a love heart. What if they fall in love? What if they get married? Flowers and hearts trail from my pen, twining between the lines. I doodle a wedding dress, sketching Treacle's head at the top, her jet black hair gathered in ringlets. As I start work on the bouquet, Jeff lets out a massive groan.

'What?' I look up.

Through the rain, I see the players clustered round the goal at the other end of the pitch.

'Tiptonville scored,' Jeff sighs.

'Does that count as an attempt on goal or a goal?' I say.

He gives me a look that could shrivel plastic. 'Goal.'

'OK.' I smile and scribble it down then go back to my bouquet and add a fringe of roses before starting work on Treacle's veil. As I lengthen the soft lace with a swirl of my pen, pooling it around her feet, the crowd roars. I look up like a startled squirrel. The Green Park players are whooping. *Goal?* I look for Treacle. She's bouncing with delight at the edge of the whoopers. Someone *must* have scored.

Then I realise Jeff's not beside me any more. Has he gone home and left me in charge of stat-logging? *Please, no!* Fear-sparks snap in my brain; I've only made three match-related notes and one of those is so entwined with roses it's hardly legible any more. I need him to fill me in on the game.

With a whoosh of relief I spot Jeff keeping pace with the linesman. He's watching the players as they fan out and restart play. Treacle punts the ball downfield. Anila heads it down and starts dribbling towards the goal. As she prepares to fire, the ref blows his whistle for half-time.

Treacle jogs over to their football coach, Miss Bayliss, who's handing out oranges to the players on the far side of the pitch. Sucking on a slice, Treacle scoops up a rain-soaked towel and wipes her blotchy, wet face.

I hurry over to Jeff. He's chatting to the linesman – Mr Chapman, my geography teacher. Glasses. Beard. Totally hopeless, but sweet. Twice a week he tries to convince me that maps hold the key to all knowledge. He hasn't won me over yet, but it's nice of him to try so hard.

'Good job Green Park equalised before half-time,' Jeff observes.

'It gives them a chance to come back.' Mr Chapman takes off his rain-spattered glasses and rubs them with the hem of his jersey.

So it *was* a goal after all. 'Who scored?' I ask innocently.

'Number seven,' Jeff answers.

*Anila.* I jot it down under the sketch of Wedding Treacle then duck between Jeff and Mr C and interrupt. 'So what do you think of the game so far?' I ask Jeff.

'Not bad.'

'Treacle's pretty fast, isn't she?'

'For a girl.'

I punch him in the arm. 'What do you mean *for a girl*?'

Jeff looks nonplussed. 'I mean she's fast for a girl. She's a top team player. Good striker too.' I make a mental note to warn Treacle that Jeff's a WYSIWYG (what you see is what you get) kind of guy. He may lack tact, but she's not going to have the hassle of second-guessing anything he says.

The ref blows his whistle and Mr Chapman starts bobbing along the sideline doing whatever it is linesmen do.

As play begins, I start doodling love hearts round the

edge of the page and, keeping one eye on the game, link them with a pretty chain of daisies. Sometimes, when I spot Treacle with the ball, I point her out to Jeff. Not too much. I don't want to make him suspicious. But I don't want him to forget she's on the field either.

As I draw a garland of buttercups round a freshly sketched heart, I wonder if Treacle will let me choose my own bridesmaid's dress. Pale green would totally highlight my eyes and I'd wear my hair up, princess-style.

'Do you take this man to be your lawfully wedded husband?'

Tears prick my eyes as Treacle passes me her bouquet and lets Jeff take her hand.

'YESSS!'

Jeff's roar makes me jump. I look up from the notepad.

'Go, Treacle!' Jeff's punching the air.

'She scored?' I stare. 'She *scored*!' Go, *Treacle!*

'The winning goal!' Jeff's clapping as the ref blows the final whistle. 'They've made it through to the next round.'

I grab his arm. 'Let's go and interview Treacle!' This is even better than I'd planned.

I don't give Jeff chance to answer, but head straight across the pitch.

Treacle's swamped by teammates, jumping round her, screaming. I wait for them to calm down, keeping one eye on Jeff in case he bolts. The rain's cleared, but the wind's still icy. I'm shivering in my duffle. This matchmaking requires commitment.

'Treacle!' I leap forward as the rest of the team head for the changing rooms. 'Great match.' I jerk my head towards Jeff, grinning. 'We've come to interview you, as you scored the winning goal and everything.' I flip over a fresh page on my notepad and wait to take notes. 'Go on,' I coax Jeff. 'Ask her what it's like to win a Cup match for your school.'

Treacle's staring at me. Is that gratitude I can see in her eyes? The wind has whipped her ponytail across her face. She looks kind of flushed and her football strip is soaked. She scrapes dripping hair away from her mouth. 'Thanks, Gem.' Her teeth are gritted against the cold.

'Nice goal,' Jeff says. 'I was beginning to think it'd go to penalties.'

'The first half was a bit scrappy.' Treacle stares at his boots.

'But you broke the deadlock.'

'It was Jing-Wei's cross that did it.'

Jeff's nodding. 'That Tiptonville defender nearly deflected it though.'

Who cares about Jing-Wei and the Tiptonville defender? He's here to interview *Treacle*. I decide to interrupt. 'Did you know Treacle's been playing football since she was three years old?'

Jeff ignores me. 'I thought you were going to score in the first five minutes,' he says. 'When you made that break.'

'Treacle's got two brothers and she can beat them both,' I interject.

Treacle's eyes are still fixed on Jeff's boots. 'I guess I didn't allow for the crosswind.'

'Crosswinds can be unpredictable,' Jeff agrees.

*Weather? What is wrong with them?* I try and steer them back on topic. 'What are your plans for tonight now you've got through to the next round?' I ask Treacle.

Treacle blinks at me. 'Homework?'

'I mean are you planning to celebrate?' *Come on, Treacle, take the hint!* 'Maybe go out somewhere? With friends? Anyone you'd like to invite?' My eyes swivel towards Jeff.

Jeff looks at me. 'Are we interviewing her about the game or planning her social diary?' He turns back to Treacle. 'Did you think the ref's decision on Erin Slater's foul was fair?'

'I don't think she meant to foul that Tiptonville winger,' Treacle answers. 'Her boot just clipped her heel as she went down.'

'Have *you* had many football injuries?' I ask Treacle. Her eyebrows shoot up.

'What about that scar on your knee you got when you were ten,' I go on. 'Why don't you show Jeff?'

Treacle backs away. 'Look, my teammates will be waiting for me.' She grabs my wrist and drags me close. 'What are you trying to do?' she hisses. 'Could you *be* more obvious?' She glances at Jeff, her face getting redder by the second. 'And why would I want to speak to him *now*? I look like I've been coughed up by a dog.'

'Sorry!' I look at Treacle's bright-red face and rain-soaked hair. Oh, no! Why didn't I think about that? 'Don't worry,' I whisper, 'I'll get rid of him.'

I pull away from Treacle and start to steer Jeff towards the sideline.

But he's already launched into another question. 'I thought Green Park had lost it at the beginning of the second half,' he says. 'When Morley latched on to that back pass from Petersen.'

'Me too,' Treacle calls over her shoulder, heading for the school. 'Good job Morley took too many touches. Anila intercepted and cleared . . .' The wind whips away the rest of her words.

I turn to Jeff. 'Great match, huh?'

'Yeah. Can I have your notes?' He holds out his hand.

'Notes?' I swallow. The doodled notepad is suddenly burning my hand. 'They're a bit scrappy. Why don't I type them up for you?'

'Don't worry.' He grabs the notepad and flicks back a page. I quietly die as he gazes at it. Hearts and flowers cover every line.

'You didn't even make a note of Slater's *foul*!' He's staring at me like I just ran over his phone.

'Sorry.' I smile sheepishly. 'The wind kept whipping my hair into my eyes and the ...' I'm fumbling for excuses. '... the rain was really ... distracting. It was kind of hard to concentrate and the doodling sort of helped me to focus I guess ...' My voice trails away. 'I'm not good with sports,' I concede.

He waves the notepad at me angrily. 'But luckily, you're great with *hearts*!'

As he turns and marches away, I huddle deeper into my duffle.

*Great with hearts?* If only that were true. He still sees Treacle as a footballer and Treacle's probably looking for another best friend right now. I get out a tissue and wipe my frozen nose. Maybe I shouldn't have tried playing Cupid after all.

'You're not working?' I dance round Dad. It's the first Saturday morning he's not worked since Christmas. Mum can't work because she needs to be at home for Ben so Dad takes all the extra shifts he can. Reality is: we need the cash, especially now Mum's thinking Ben should have a maths tutor because he's missed out on so much school.

'He's not working!' Excited, I leap across the sofa, bowling Ben into the soft cushions. 'Did you hear that, Ben? We've got Dad all Saturday!'

Ben whoops with delight and struggles out from under me. 'Can we go swimming?' He rushes over to Dad. Ben loves swimming, which is great because the fitter he gets, the fitter he stays.

'Who wants a fried egg sandwich?' Mum pops her head round the kitchen door.

'Me!' Ben and Dad chorus at once.

'Me too!' I chime in.

'Can we go swimming once we've eaten?' Ben looks eagerly at Dad.

'We could go later while Gemma's in town with Treacle,' Dad suggests.

Treacle's forgiven me for embarrassing her in front of Jeff. It didn't take much. 'I guess your heart was in the right place,' she conceded after I'd waited for her outside the changing room and gushed a few hundred apologies.

Dad looks at me. 'Is that OK with you, Gem?'

'Yes!' We get the whole morning together; then Ben gets some precious one-on-one time with Dad while I go for lunch and then check out the sale at Mizz-tique with Treacle. Win-win.

We eat the sandwiches, then I play football in the back garden with Ben and Dad. They teach me about fouls and free kicks and attempts on goal and corners. I want to prove to Jeff I'm not just a moony dweeb.

I frown at Dad as I grapple with the concept of 'offside'. 'So if the player gets the ball and there's no defenders between him and the goal, it's offside?' I'm determined to understand. Jeff *has* to take me seriously if I'm ever going to sell him on Treacle. 'Doesn't that make it harder?'

'That's the point,' Dad explains.

Frustration flickers through me. Selling Treacle shouldn't be this much work; Treacle rocks! Why's Jeff so blind? It must be his Year Ten goggles. They screen out Year Nines like sunglasses screen out UV.

Ben's out of breath, but we keep on playing till Mum calls us in.

'It's too cold,' she worries, wrapping Ben in a jumper as soon as he gets through the door.

'I'm boiling!' he says, fighting it off.

'Let's give him a couple of minutes to cool down and then he can put it on,' I suggest.

'Yeah!' Ben heads for the TV. 'Do you want to watch cartoons, Gem?'

'You bet.' I grab the jumper off Mum and dive for the sofa, bagging the best corner while Ben flicks through the channels.

It's gone quiet in the kitchen. I bet Mum and Dad are smooching. 'Turn the sound up a bit,' I tell Ben. 'Unless you want to hear the old folk snogging.'

'Ew!' he snorts and ratchets up the volume.

We watch cartoons till Dad appears like a genie (without a lamp) at the end of the sofa. He's crept up quiet as a cat and is wearing a big grin as he rustles Ben's swimming bag. 'Ready to go?' he says loudly.

'Argh!' Ben bashes against me, squawking with surprise.

'One point to me, I think,' Dad announces with satisfaction. 'That makes it 74–70.'

Dad and Ben have this ongoing game called Ninja

Attack. They get points if they manage to creep up on someone and score a surprise. Dad is currently winning, which has made Ben über-competitive. The only safe place in the house now is the bathroom. Or next to Mum. Mum's banned them from creeping up on her; she's dropped too many plates.

Ben's still grumbling that Dad's cheated as Dad ushers him out of the front door.

'Do you want a lift?' Dad jingles his car keys at me.

I shake my head. 'No thanks. I'm meeting Treacle on the bus.'

I check my watch. I've got half an hour to persuade my hair to cooperate and disguise the zit that's threatening to erupt on my chin. I move like lightning up to my bedroom, wriggle into my skinny jeans and pull on my favourite hooded top before nearly losing a comb in my hair. I make it to the bus stop, brushed, dusted and booted, just as the number 38 comes grumbling into view.

I wave it down and hop onboard. On the top deck I'm pleased to see the front seats are empty. I slide on to one and relish the massive view as the bus bounces down the road.

Treacle's waiting at the next stop. She's just a speck when I spot her. I start waving. My hand aches by the time the bus shudders to a halt next to her. She looks different. No football jersey. No joggers. And is she wearing a *skirt*? I turn in my seat and wait, holding my breath. A moment later, her glossy black hair appears, bobbing up the stairs. She swings into the seat beside me. I do a double take.

'OMG! You're wearing make-up!' I think that Treacle always looks pretty, but today she's looking prettier than ever. I take in the rest of her outfit. 'And a skirt?' An *above-the-knee* skirt too! With thick tights and fringed boots that match her jacket.

She's blushing. 'Do I look OK?'

'You look gorgeous!'

She gives a self-conscious smile and I change the subject before I kill the moment with kindness.

We get off the bus near the town hall and dodge through the crowds towards our favourite coffee shop, an olde worlde café with the best home-made cakes ever.

'Can I have two slices of chocolate cake, please and one half-fat cinnamon latte.' I lay my money on the counter. 'And a mocha frappuccino.' I order for Treacle, then hesitate. 'That's still your favourite, right?' New babe-alicious Treacle might have changed her taste in coffee and cake as well as clothes.

She swings her hair back over her shoulder. 'Of course.'

We sit at the window, watching the Saturday shoppers stream past.

'Why couldn't Savannah come shopping with us?'

'Why do you think?' Treacle stirs her frappuccino. 'She's seeing a movie with Josh this afternoon.'

Savannah always disappears from the scene when she's snagged a new boy. 'What's the movie?'

'A rom-com, I think.'

'Ah, so I'm guessing Savannah chose it?' I smile and take a sip from my coffee, nearly choking as I spot Sam outside on the pavement. He's clutching a handful of leaflets and thrusting them at passers-by.

'What?' Treacle follows my gaze.

'Don't look, but Cindy's deep-dish is leafleting outside the window.'

Treacle looks, *of course*, and her stare seems to attract Sam. He peers through the window and I feel an electric jolt of surprise as his eye catches mine. This is becoming a horrible habit. I focus quickly on my latte, hoping he doesn't think I stare at him as a hobby. Next minute he's heading for the door of the coffee shop.

I hunch harder over my coffee, wondering what he wants. Perhaps he's going to ask me for some editorial assistance with his flyers?

'Hi, Gemma.' He stops beside our table. 'Hi, Treacle.'

*He knows her name.* I look up. He knows her *nickname*. I wish all Year Tens were as thoughtful as Sam.

'You're looking nice.' He grins at Treacle, his blue eyes lighting up. I break into a smile, pleased for Treacle.

76

Pulling off a makeover takes guts and I'm glad Sam's given her the seal of approval. 'What are the leaflets for?' I peer at the papers drooping in his hand, trying to read upside down.

'My band's doing a gig tonight.' He thumbs off a couple and hands them to me. 'Why don't you come?'

I swap glances with Treacle. Her new look is already getting results. 'Do you want to go?' I ask her. *Please say yes!* I silently plead. A Year Ten gig is way too cool to miss.

'Yes!' she replies and Sam's immediately grinning again.

I smile up at him, but my lips freeze as I see Cindy loom over his shoulder. Where did she come from? I check behind her, half expecting to see a puff of smoke, but there's only Barbara. The two of them are loaded with shopping bags. 'What's this about a gig?' Cindy uses her gooey voice on Sam, throwing dagger-stares at me. She reaches round and slips a leaflet from his hand, letting her silky hair slide past his cheek. 'Is this your band? Cool.' She glances at Barbara. 'Shall we go to this?'

I look at Sam. He must be flattered. But he's just shrugging. 'Yeah, great.'

Cindy scans the coffee shop. 'Come on, Barbara, let's head to Starbucks.' She stuffs Sam's flyer into her handbag. 'This place is a bit too quaint for me.' She tips her head towards Sam. 'Do you want to come with us?'

Sam waves his bunch of flyers at her. 'Sorry, Cindy. I promised the rest of the band I'd get rid of these.'

'Oh, well, see you later then.' Cindy shimmers away, Barbara waving goodbye as she hurries after.

'Then you're coming tonight?' Sam says, looking at us.

Treacle nods. 'Can we invite our friend Savannah too?'

'Sure.' He heads for the door and a moment later he's back on the pavement, flapping leaflets at shoppers.

'He's cute.' Treacle's eyes are shining in my direction.

'Cindy certainly thinks he is.'

'What about you?'

'Well, duh!' I glance through the window. The cold January wind is tousling Sam's shaggy hair. It's *so* not fair that a breeze which turns him windswept would froth my hair into a style only the wild beast of Borneo would choose. 'But he's a Year Ten. A totally *DD* Year Ten, and Cindy's got him in her sights.' I sigh, and start doing some sums in my head. I calculate that it'll take Cindy a week to get Sam on a date and a fortnight to make him her boyfriend. Add a year of fluttering eyelashes and she'll own him for life.

While Treacle texts the good news about tonight's plans to Savannah, I slump over my coffee and take a sip. It's frothy and hot and sweet.

'I've told her to meet us on the eight-thirty bus,' Treacle says, putting her phone back into her bag. We finish our coffee and cake and head for Mizz-tique. We time it just right. The shopping herd has cleared out all of the dull stock and left only the precious gems. You need excellent taste to appreciate them.

'This would really suit you.' I grab a frou-frou dress from the rail and hold it against Treacle. The dark red ruffles look stunning against her black hair and olive skin. But I can tell from the look on her face that she's not ready for frills yet. 'OK.' I give in gracefully and put it back on the rail. 'Keep it simple.' I browse for myself, knowing instinctively when my gaze falls on a dusky pink top with a butterfly motif that my search is over.

I try it on, Treacle nodding, suitably impressed. Then I pay and let Treacle run her finger across a few rails before she decides on a tartan mini-kilt. I encourage her, sensing she's still self-conscious about her style change.

'You are going to look great in it,' I promise. 'Even Savannah's going to be jealous.'

'Really?' She looks at me anxiously.

'Definitely.' With Treacle's football-toned legs, there's no doubt about it.

We browse a few more shops before catching the bus home. As it hisses and whines its way along the road, we plan our night at Sam's gig.

'Are you going to wear your new kilt?' I ask, hoping for a yes. 'I'm definitely wearing the top I bought.'

'What are you going to wear it with?' Treacle doesn't answer the kilt question and I decide not to push it. She has to make the long journey to babedom at her own speed. Too fast and she may have a fashion breakdown. My memory wanders back to the time that Ryan from our form decided to go emo. One Monday he was denim and long crew cut, the next he was black duster coat and drooping fringe. Brave look for a boy who wears glasses and rides a mountain bike, but he couldn't follow through. By Friday he was back in denim and cracking jokes at the back of the class.

'Ground control calling Gemma.' Treacle snaps her fingers in my face. 'Come in, Gemma.'

'What?' I snap back to the present.

'What are you going to wear with the new top?'

'Oh. Jeans I s'pose.'

'Not something more glam?' Treacle tempts me. 'There'll probably be lots of boys there.'

'Oh God – Jeff might be there!' I look at Treacle excitedly. 'Maybe Sam's invited everyone who works on the webzine.'

Treacle twitches then slumps. 'I don't think he's into indie rock,' she sighs.

I shrug. 'You never know.'

We stare in hopeful silence as Treacle's stop swings into view. She grabs her shopping bags and gets to her feet.

'You'll be round at mine at seven?' she calls over her shoulder as she heads for the stairs.

'Definitely!' I call back. 'We'll need at least an hour to get ready!'

As Treacle hops out of the bus on to the grass verge, I wave at her. Excitement's fizzing through me. We're going to a real live gig. I wonder what Sam's band will be like? Will there be other kids from school apart from Cindy? Will my hair stay straight all night? Jeans or skirt?

I'm so lost in thought, I almost miss my stop and have to hammer down the stairs in time to catch the driver's eye. He screeches to a halt and I thank him breathlessly as I jump off.

I walk home, swinging my Mizz-tique bag by its string handle. My new top is low cut. Dad's going to hate it. It'll be perfect for tonight. I hurry up the front path.

'Hi!' I call as I let myself in.

'Hi, love,' Mum calls from the living room. I go through and find her with her feet up in front of the TV. A black-and-white movie's flickering on-screen. 'Dad and Ben should be back soon,' she says, taking a handful of crisps from a bowl on her lap. I can't remember the last time I saw Mum looking so relaxed.

I plump down next to her, swinging my Mizz-tique bag on to my knee. 'Guess what—' I'm about to tell her about the gig, but she mutes the TV and turns to face me. She's suddenly looking worried. I frown. 'Is everything OK?'

'Oh, yes, everything's fine,' she says quickly. 'I just wanted to ask a favour.'

'Sure.'

'Will you babysit Ben tonight?' Her eyes are round and hopeful.

'Tonight?' My heart steps up to the edge of a cliff and prepares to dive.

'Ben's so well at the moment. He hasn't had a chest infection for ages. And he's been putting on weight and sleeping well. Me and your dad thought – since we don't have to worry so much about him right now – you could sit with him while we went out.'

I let the Mizz-tique bag slide off my lap. 'Oh.'

'We'll only be gone a couple of hours.' Her eyes are searching mine anxiously.

Guilt swamps me. 'Of course.' Mum and Dad never get to have a night out together. They're usually too tired or too worried about money. I can't let them down. And it's not as if we can leave Ben with anyone. There's his night time routine – the nebulizer and the physio. I force a smile. 'I'd be happy to.'

Mum's face lights up like she's won the lottery. 'Really?'

'Sure.' My heart's dived and is plummeting towards the rocks. But I keep my smile going. 'I can catch up with some schoolwork.'

'Can't Treacle come over?' Mum's looking worried again.

I shake my head. 'She's busy.' My heart splatters on the rocks as I realise I've got to break the news to Treacle.

I flip out my phone and start composing a text. *Sorry, Treacle, can't come to gig. Mum and Dad need me to babysit tonight x*

She answers straight away. *No!!!!* ☹

I text back. *U can still go with Sav and maybe Jeff will be there x*

OK. Her reply feels less than enthusiastic. *But it won't be the same w/o u.*

I glance round the sitting room. The coffee table's crowded with cups. A crumby plate is balancing on the arm of the sofa; Dad left it there after shovelling in a quick snack before leaving.

I could tidy up.

I'm trying to keep the one thought out of my head that most wants to be there. The thought that Treacle and Savannah will be getting ready for a night of fun at Sam's gig.

How is that fair?

Ben needs me here, I remind myself. Mum and Dad deserve a night out. I check on Ben again. He's sound asleep, flat out and angel-faced. I wander back to the living room and start to gather up some mugs.

My mind slips back to my webzine assignment. I bet Jessica Jupiter wouldn't be tidying up. An image shimmers into my mind. I see a woman – half Miss Duvall, a ballet teacher I used to have, and half Bette Davis, an actress in the old black-and-white movies that my mum loves. The woman I'm imagining has bobbed platinum hair, scarlet fingernails like bloody daggers, a cocktail dress and heels. She's firing words like a machine gun, simultaneously ordering someone else to clear away the mess while composing next week's horoscopes.

'*Darling.*' I let the mugs clatter back on to the coffee table and address the empty lounge. 'I see your future before me.' I lift my chin and stand on tiptoe like I'm wearing four-inch stilettos. 'And honey, you'd better duck because it's coming at you fast.'

I smile. Being Jessica Jupiter might not be so bad after all, as long as no one walks in and finds me talking to myself. I scuff across the carpet, my puppy-faced slippers peeping out from under my jeans. My backpack is leaning against the bookcase. I rummage through it and drag out my jotter.

Flopping down on to the sofa, I put my feet up and rest the notepad on my knees. I reach for the pen I know will be tangled in my hair. This is the *only thing* curly hair is good for – pen storage. I slide out a purple sparkly gel pen from somewhere at the back.

Leo

I underline it.

<u>Leo</u>

*What a week you have in store!*

I frown. What else? You'll be kidnapped by aliens? You'll win the lottery? I could make anything up.

What would Jessica Jupiter write? She wouldn't be

*writing* for a start; she'd be dictating to a humble secretary. I picture Jessica seated at her dressing table like Miss Duvall getting ready for a performance. Jessica's dabbing her nose with a big white puff, the fur-edged sleeves of her gown swirling face powder into clouds. Her secretary leans forward on a footstool, quietly choking in the dust-haze while scribbling on to a pad.

*So you think you're king of the jungle, Leo?*

Jessica's dictating. I'm scribbling.

*Well, you're right! Don't be afraid to show your teeth. You are the* mane *player in this week's drama.*

Mum's mobile suddenly beeps. I look up, surprised. Didn't she take it with her? I spot it sitting in the fruit bowl. Mum's always picking up the wrong thing by mistake. There's probably an apple in her handbag.

It gives me an idea.

*Keep your phone close at hand this week, Simba. Someone will want to contact you with news, which might turn out to be surprisingly fruitful. On Friday . . .*

I spot the corner of the rug, rucked up like a mini mountain range, just waiting to trip someone.

*. . . you'll get news of an unexpected trip. Pack everything, Star-ling. You may need to dress to impress.*

*The weekend will bring . . .*

I bite my lip, thinking hard. The DVDs piled next to the telly catch my eye.

. . . *a titanic opportunity. Make the most of it, Leo, and you'll start next week, not just as a lion, but as a lion king.*

I stop feeling like the secretary and start feeling like Jessica. I grin. Writing these horoscopes might actually be fun.

*Libra*

*Your star-sign may be the Scales, but your life is not as well-balanced as it might seem. Star-ling, don't despair.*

Outside an ambulance shrieks past, making my heart race.

*A shock is in store, but take deep breaths and stay focused on the job at hand. You work as hard as you play, my sweet, so when the scales start to tip in your favour, they'll tip big time.*

I glance at the cluster of dirty mugs on the coffee table. *Meanwhile, a mess you should have cleared up ages ago will come back to haunt you, but handle it right and you can turn the mess into a triumph.*

I push a cushion behind my head and snuggle deeper into the sofa.

*Rest at the weekend.*

I search the room for more inspiration. *Watch TV. Read a book. Think of it as the calm before the storm – but don't worry; you have the heart of a Libran, not a librarian. You're going to enjoy the storm!*

*Virgo*

The only person I know who is a Virgo is Susan Noakes, the quietest girl in our class.

*You're the most timid of all my Star-lings, Virgo, but this week you're going to turn shy into shine . . .*

I glance at the CD rack.

*Take inspiration from your musical heroes and step up to the microphone of life.*

I write for an hour until I've just got one horoscope left.

<u>Pisces</u>

I roll my pen thoughtfully in my fingers and catch sight of my fingernails, bitten and bare. Jessica Jupiter would be ashamed. I vow to stop biting them. I've vowed to stop biting them four million times before, but this time I mean it.

*This is going to be quite a week for you, my fishy friend.*

What can I write? I look around for more inspiration. Jessica's used just about every piece of furniture and ornament in the room. She's run out of words. There's only hash symbols and asterisks left in her head. I suck on my pen.

*It may start duller than a wet Sunday.*

I catch sight of one of my dad's CD cases next to the stereo.

*You may feel as inspired as a seventy-year-old rock star but just wait . . .*

I see a photo of my cousin, Jen.

*. . . an unexpected visit from a relative . . .*

Mum's light-up globe is sitting on the bookcase.

*. . . from overseas will bring . . .*

What?

An armchair?

A bowl of potpourri?

Dad's plate? I stare at it blankly. The cheddar crumbs have dried up and turned transparent.

*. . . cheese.*

An *unexpected visit from a relative from overseas will bring* cheese? Jessica must be delirious from overwork, but it'll have to do.

I shut my jotter, deciding to type up the horoscopes after a healthy dose of TV. But as I reach for the remote, the phone rings. I leap up and answer it before it wakes Ben.

'Gemma?'

'Treacle? Aren't you supposed to be at the gig?'

I can practically *hear* Treacle smiling. 'I got ready and found bus money and then thought, what fun will it be without Gem?'

'But what about Savannah?'

'She's coming too. We're your best friends, Gem, we can't leave you home alone on a Saturday night – we would be failing in our BFF duties. '

I grin madly, even though I know that only a six-year-old is supposed to be ridiculously pleased that her best friends can't have fun without her.

Treacle carries on. 'So Savannah's picking up some pizza and I'm bringing the new Jack Black movie. Are you up for it?'

'Totally!' I squeal.

I hang up after about a million byes, then go and throw a bag of popcorn in the microwave. After all, with pizza, you always need dessert.

The last bell rings, signalling the end of Monday's lessons. I wait for the OK from Mr Chapman then stuff my geography book in my bag. The webzine deadline meeting starts in five minutes.

'Are you sure you don't want to walk with me to webzine HQ?' I ask Treacle.

Treacle's stuffing her rucksack. 'I'm sure.'

'We might bump into Jeff on the way.'

'*Exactly.*'

I coax harder. 'You can showcase your new look.' Today Treacle is even wearing a little bit of make-up to school. I'd have been less surprised if Mr Chapman had turned up in mascara.

Treacle gives me a look; it's the same look she gave me when we were eight and I gave her liquorice. 'Gemma.' She tips her head. 'Are you trying to kill me?'

'What?'

'I would *die* of embarrassment if Jeff saw me.'

'Why?'

'I don't work on the webzine. It'll look really weird.'

'No, it won't. It'll just look like you're hanging out.'

'Outside the storeroom?' Treacle yelps.

'It's fine. Even if we do bump into Jeff, he won't know you're there because of *him*,' I reason.

Treacle slings her bag over her shoulder. 'You're right, Gemma,' she says. 'He could think I hang around outside the storeroom waiting for *anyone* – and that wouldn't be embarrassing at all!'

I catch up with her thought-train. 'Oh.'

She ruffles my hair fondly. 'Thanks for trying, Gem.' She heads for the door. 'I'll phone you later.'

The corridors are awash with kids pouring out of their last lessons. I dart like a fish through the flood and fight my way upstream towards the webzine HQ. Cindy's already behind her desk. Can this girl time-travel as well? I scan the room for a teleport. 'How did you get here so fast?'

'Free period.' She drops her voice. 'I got your piece by the way.' I'd emailed her Jessica's horoscopes before school. 'They were a little—' she stops for a suitably dramatic pause, '—eccentric. But not too bad for a first effort,' she concedes.

'Thanks.'

'But don't forget.' She taps a pile of papers together. 'This is just between us.'

'Yeah.' I slide behind a PC. As I drop my schoolbag on the empty chair beside me, Sam breezes in.

'Are you saving that seat for me?' He teases me like I'm an equal, not an age-deprived charity case.

'It's for Will actually,' I shoot back. 'You know how much he loves Year Nines.'

Cindy flutters out from behind her desk and perches on the front of it. 'Great gig on Saturday, Sam. You were brilliant.'

'I guess it went OK.' Sam scratches his head. 'We need more practise really.' He looks at me. 'What did you think?'

I shrug apologetically. 'I couldn't make it in the end. Sorry.'

'Oh.' Sam turns away and dumps his bag. His shoulders are drooping like he's had a long day.

Suddenly Cindy's flapping papers in my face. 'Here.' I take them before she slices off my nose.

She hands another wad to Sam. 'I've printed out everyone's articles. I thought we could all read them and check for mistakes.'

I quickly scan the sheets and see Jessica Jupiter's name above the horoscopes. I'm in print! Or rather *Jessica's* in print. Joy and despair duel like musketeers round my heart.

'*We're* reading them?' Sam raises an eyebrow. 'I thought editing was your job.'

Cindy smiles sweetly. 'You can't expect the editor-in-chief to do all of the proofreading, Sam. And besides, I want everyone to feel part of the process.'

The door squeaks as Phil and David file in. Jeff's right behind them. As they all grab seats, I slide down in my chair, wilting with embarrassment as I remember my heart-themed notes from the football match, but Jeff doesn't look at me.

'Hey, David,' he says, his foot tapping restlessly. 'Did you see the match on Saturday?'

David shakes his head and Phil answers. 'We were at Comic-Con.'

Jeff sits bolt upright. 'I forgot!' His face is suddenly wide awake, like he's been kissed by Princess Charming. 'How was it? I went last year. Got Dave Gibbons's autograph.'

'Dave Gibbons?' Phil's in awe. 'No way.'

'Uh-huh.'

Sam's head snaps round. 'Commy-what?'

'Comic Book Convention,' Jeff explains.

My ears prick up. Treacle's always got an X-Men comic in her bag. Maybe she should start carrying it in the open. If Jeff's into comics, a glimpse of Wolverine in the lunch hall might act like catnip. In my head he's already jumping dining tables to sit beside Treacle. Their eyes meet as he points a trembling finger at Magneto leering from the cover. 'You like X-Men?' he whispers.

Treacle slides her 1984 original *Spiderman and the Mighty Thor* out of her bag and wafts it seductively under Jeff's nose. Hypnotised, he leans in for a kiss . . .

'Hello, everyone,' Barbara calls out breathlessly as she

enters the room, fishing for something in her bag. She takes a seat beside Cindy and smiles broadly as she hooks out a pen.

Next Will swaggers in and parks himself on top of Sam's desk, slouching against the monitor.

'So?' He eyes Cindy. 'Was my piece OK?'

'You mean your article?' Cindy starts handing out papers to everyone. 'Why don't we all decide?'

'So we're a democracy now?' Will's eyes are as sharp as switchblades. I'm suddenly relieved it's Jessica's name at the top of the horoscopes, not mine.

The room grows quiet as we start reading this week's edition. The only sound is Cindy's pen scratching notes in the margin. My gaze drifts over the first article.

*Twenty Ways to Get the Most From Your School Locker.*

This is Barbara's feature article! My brain flip-flops like a stunned fish.

*Twenty Ways to Get the Most From Your School Locker?*

She calls this *lifestyle*? Death-by-boredom-style more like!

Frustration chokes me. Why am I inventing horoscopes under someone else's name while Barbara gets a byline for this?

Will's smirking. 'Nice piece, Barbara. I think you've changed my life.' He holds up his paper and reads aloud. 'A neat locker is a sweet locker.'

Barbara beams. 'Thanks, Will.'

Jeff looks up. 'Keeping muddy kit at the bottom is actually a good idea,' he says kindly.

'Genius,' Will mutters.

Cindy shushes him and we all continue to read, marking up any typos as we go. When we've finished, Cindy starts collecting the papers in. But when she gets to Will, he waves his in front of her. 'Have you *actually* read any of this, Cindy?'

I glue my gaze to my lap, but I can feel Cindy's rage sparking across the room.

'Of course I have, Will,' she snarls. 'I've read everything and I think it's great.'

'Great? This Jessica Jupiter person is a total airhead.' I flinch as Will flicks past my column and runs through the rest of the pages. 'And as for the rest of it. "Lip gloss – or lip matte – you decide." *Girls'* football?' He pauses as though he can't believe what he's reading. 'I thought we were publishing a student webzine not a Girl Guide manual.' He slings his papers at Cindy. 'What about addressing real issues?'

Cindy glares at him. 'And your piece on student loans is a *real* issue?'

'Of course it is!'

Cindy slams the papers on her desk and puts her hands on her hips. She clearly means business. 'Have you studied our demographic? This is a *secondary* school not higher education.'

Jeff interrupts. 'It's only the first issue. I'm sure it'll improve.'

Will and Cindy turn their headlight glares on him.

'You don't like it either?' Cindy snaps.

Will growls. 'You were *expecting* it to be bad?'

Jeff holds up his hands like he's deflecting goals. 'Whoa!'

Cindy takes a breath. 'Well, perhaps Mr Harris's idea isn't such a bad one after all.'

Will narrows his eyes. 'What idea?'

'He wants us to invite our readers to submit their own articles for the next issue to run alongside ours.' She looks like she's licked a frog.

Will rolls his eyes. 'Great,' he growls. 'Let the masses speak. They've always got so *much* to say.' His words drip with sarcasm.

I press my lips together, squashing a smile. It looks like Will and Cindy have something in common after all. They both think their readers are pond life.

Cindy's eyes brighten unconvincingly. 'What do you all think?'

I think that maybe if more people are going to be contributing to the webzine then Cindy might consider my piece about the school shed.

Sam swings his feet on to his desk. 'We might get some interesting stuff.'

'Dream on,' Will mutters.

But David's nodding. 'It's worth a try.'

Phil's typing on his keyboard. 'Collaboration built the internet,' he says, not looking up from his screen.

The school shed idea is now disco-dancing in my head. I could have a chance to get it published after all.

Cindy bites her bottom lip. 'If people wanted to *collaborate*, they should have come to the first meeting and joined up.' She flicks back her hair. 'But Mr Harris thinks it's a good idea, so I'll be sending out an appeal for articles with the first issue.'

I clear my throat. 'Cindy, I have an idea too. What about an article about the demolition of the bike shed and how it will affect the students who use it for – you know – *other* activities?' I stop there, praying that my cheeks don't start to burn.

Barbara giggles and Will sighs. Sam looks at me and grins.

Cindy holds up a hand. 'The ideas are meant to come from the readers, not us.' She turns and starts thrusting papers into her bag. 'We might as well close the meeting. Let's meet again on Thursday to start work on the next issue.'

She marches out of the room, Barbara chasing after, her schoolbag flapping behind.

Will heaves himself to his feet and leaves. Sam, Phil and David are quick to follow. Cindy and Will's argument seems to have left everyone a little shell-shocked. I bend down to fetch my bag from under the desk.

'I like your idea.' Jeff's voice makes me jump. He's in front of my desk, shifting his feet like the floor's too hot.

'Thanks.' I grab my bag and stand up, ready to leave. It's not Jeff I need to sell my idea to, it's the Ice Queen.

'Sorry.' Jeff's still staring at me.

'What for?'

'For being uncool about your . . .' His gaze darts to his feet. '. . . drawings.'

The flowers and hearts! In all the tension of the meeting I'd completely forgotten. 'No! *I'm* sorry!' I blurt. 'I should've written down the goals and stuff.'

'Doesn't matter.' Jeff looks at me. 'I'd logged the stats in my head anyway.'

'Really?' I'm impressed.

'Anyway, I'm sorry I snapped at you. I was just caught up in the game,' Jeff continues.

I shrug. 'It's OK.'

He's shifting his feet again. 'That bike shed article is a good idea,' he tells me again. And then he's gone. Out of the door like a rabbit running for a gap in the fence.

OMG. I realise in a flash.

He's *shy*! He only really knows how to talk about sport. I'm scribbling mental notes to Treacle. This is great news. No wonder he's not asked her out yet. This is going to be easy! Treacle talks sports like Savannah talks fashion. She and Jeff are made for each other. I can't wait to tell her.

I hurry out of school and cross the playground. The bike shed looks shadowy in the late afternoon light. I stare at the tarmac, irritated as I think of Cindy batting my idea away. My Save Our Shed piece would have blown Barbara's locker drivel out of the water. The shed is something the students *really* care about. I hunch my shoulders against the cold. Then I hear voices.

Someone's behind the shed.

Isn't it a bit late for a romantic rendezvous? The yard's deserted and the cleaners are in full swing inside, their hoovers echoing along the halls. Curious, I creep towards the back of the shed. The voices sound familiar. I peep round the corner, squinting through the shadows.

*Josh?*

I recognise his jacket. And his dark curls. He's in a passionate clinch.

*Savannah?* I peer harder.

That's not Savannah! My heart lurches.

It's Chelsea.

Josh is snogging Chelsea!

'We have to tell her,' Treacle insists as we head up the school steps.

It's Wednesday and I still haven't told Savannah about Josh. The sun's out, pretending nothing's wrong, but there's a sharp nip in the cold morning air.

'Can't we just let her find out by herself?' I push through the front doors. 'She's so happy.'

'And let Josh get away with two-timing?'

I know she's right, but I really don't want to be the one to capsize Savannah's love boat.

'Savannah's going to get hurt whatever,' Treacle points out. 'If he's already cheating on her then it's only going to get worse.'

Registration sucks.

I scowl at Josh as he drapes himself round Savannah. He's got one eye on Chelsea, who's chewing gum on the other side of the classroom.

'I'm going to tell Savannah at break-time,' I whisper to Treacle as the bell goes for the first lesson.

'We'll do it together,' Treacle hisses back.

Mr Harris catches my eye as I walk into English. 'Good first effort,' he smiles.

'Sorry?'

'The webzine,' he explains. 'I enjoyed reading it.'

I've been so wrapped up in Savannah's heartbreak that I've totally forgotten that the webzine goes public today. It'll be in everyone's Inbox by now.

Treacle grabs my arm as we take our seats. 'The webzine! I forgot!'

'Me too!' I wish I had a smartphone so I could check my email.

Behind me, Savannah leans over her desk. 'I'm going to check it out at break,' she whispers. 'We can go to the IT suite. I must see Cindy's beauty tips.' She giggles. 'I want to find out what she uses to freeze her smile.'

I try and focus on Mr Harris. He's snapped open a copy of *To Kill a Mockingbird* and started droning.

As soon as the bell goes for break, I drag Treacle to the IT suite. Savannah and Sally Moore have got there before us and are already at two of the computers.

I'm bouncing with excitement as I type in my password. I'm about to finally see my words in print!

Suddenly Savannah explodes into laughter.

Treacle looks at her. 'What?'

Savannah's creased up, pointing at the screen. 'Who is Jessica Jupiter?'

Sally's giggling beside her. 'She's crazy!'

Savannah starts reading out my horoscopes. Her voice chokes with laughter. 'An unexpected visit from a relative from overseas will bring *cheese*!' She collapses, hooting, against Sally.

I feel sick. My cheeks are on fire, my stomach as hollow as an empty locker.

What a great start to my career.

I grab my bag and head for the door. 'I've got to go, I'm feeling sick,' I somehow manage to blurt out on the way.

'Wait!' Treacle's hot on my heels.

I race from the IT suite. 'I'm so embarrassed!' I clutch Treacle's arm. 'You must promise *never* to tell anyone that it's me!'

'I know.' Treacle's nodding. 'I swear on my mother's chimichangas.' Her eyes search mine hopefully. She's trying to make me laugh.

I droop. I don't feel like laughing. 'The whole school will be making fun of me by the end of the day.'

'They don't know it's *you* who wrote it.' Treacle puts her arm through mine and leads me down the corridor. 'You did the best you could but it was never meant to be serious, was it?'

'I guess not,' I conceded. But it would have been nice

if Savannah had just smiled instead of falling off her chair in hysterics.

'I'm resigning,' I tell Treacle as we cross the playground the next morning. A cold February mist has swallowed the school roof.

'Resigning?' Treacle's shoes clip-clop on the front steps. 'From what? *School?*' She sounds hopeful. 'I didn't know you could resign from school.'

A reluctant smile twitches my lips. 'Not school. The webzine.' I spent yesterday evening working myself into a full-blown huff. 'If Cindy won't take me seriously then there's no point,' I sniff. 'Writing horoscopes is humiliating. It's a sell-out. I should be writing serious pieces about serious things.'

Treacle's frowning. 'But you were really looking forward to working on the webzine,' she reminds me. 'Shouldn't you give it a bit longer?'

I barge through the school doors and plunge into the crowd of students. 'I'm not being the school laughing stock,' I call over my shoulder as Treacle squeezes after me.

She stops arguing as we focus on making it to the classroom without getting trampled. Savannah's already there, perched on a desk. Sal, Anila and Susan Noakes are clustered round her. Even Chelsea's crowding to hear.

'I couldn't believe it!' Savannah exclaims. 'I got home

from school last night and my Uncle Pierre was sat at the kitchen table. He'd come on a surprise visit from France. Even Mum didn't know he was coming. And guess what he brought as a gift?'

Anila's leaning forward. 'What?'

'*Cheese!*'

Sal's the first to burst into laughter. 'So Jessica Jupiter was right!'

'A hundred and ten per cent!' Savannah exclaims. 'She really is psychic!'

I'm standing in the doorway, eyes wide.

Treacle squeezes my arm. 'How did you know he was coming?'

'I didn't!' I hush her before she gives anything away.

Jessica's prediction actually came true! I couldn't be more amazed if Miss Davis climbed on her desk and started tap-dancing.

Savannah and the others are speed-talking about Jessica Jupiter and her horoscopes. They sound as excited as nerds in an Apple store. Do they actually believe Jessica's predictions are real?

An idea lights up my head.

'Treacle!' I drag her to our usual spot beside the radiator.

'What?' Her gaze is darting between me and Savannah.

'I've just worked out how we can warn Savannah about Josh!'

I don't resign. In fact, at lunchtime I can't wait to get to webzine HQ and start work on next week's horoscopes.

If Savannah believes in Jessica Jupiter, I can let Jessica break the bad news about Josh. Jessica's way tougher than me. She'll find a way to get her message across.

I hurry past the staffroom, heading for the stairs. Mr Chapman's outside talking to Miss Bayliss, our PE teacher.

'Well Jeff Simpson seemed very keen when he watched the girls' Cup match,' Mr Chapman's saying. 'Maybe you should ask him.'

I slow down, ears pricking like a cat's. Ask him what?

Miss Bayliss starts to smile. 'Oh, yes, he'd make a perfect coach for the Year Nine girls' team. He's such a great player, they'd really look up to him.'

*I know one of them would.* Even as I'm thinking it, another thought's running in my head: *this is GREAT info.* My mind starts whirring; if I can get Jeff to believe in his horoscope then, with a couple of flicks of Jessica Jupiter's pen, I can steer him towards Treacle, in the same way that I can warn Savannah not to trust Josh. I just need to word the horoscopes carefully. I'm such an Evil Genius, I should have my own comic book.

*Gemma Stone is the Dark Writer! With her mighty Pen of Destiny – sharper than any sword, stronger than any fist – the Dark Writer is the only Evil Genius who can rewrite the future before it's even happened.*

Miss Bayliss glances at her watch. 'When I get a spare moment, I'll ask him if he'll do it.'

I sidle past, eyes fixed on the floor, already typing Jeff's horoscope in my head. *Expect an unexpected offer . . .*

Sam, Cindy and Will are already in the storeroom. Sam's lost in music, eyes closed, biting his lip as he nods along to the MP3 player wired into his ears. Cindy's typing. She doesn't even look up as I enter. Will's copying something from his screen on to a notepad beside his keyboard. I sit down and start up a PC.

'Gemma?'

I look up and jerk back in surprise as I see Cindy leaning over my desk.

This girl moves like a ninja.

'Y-yes?'

A horrible mish-mash of fumes washes over me. Mouthwash, face powder, hairspray and perfume battle for supremacy in my nose. I fight back a sneeze, eyes smarting.

'How did you get on with those samples I gave you?' she asks, loud enough to rattle the windows.

I guess she's still pushing the idea that I'm helping her with her beauty column. 'Fine,' I tell her unenthusiastically.

'Well?' Her gaze is flitting over my desk. 'Where are they? I'm not just giving you free stuff, you know.'

Beside me, Will shifts in his seat. 'I can't imagine you giving anything away for free, Cinders.'

She lasers him with a look. '*Don't* call me Cinders.'

His lips twitch and I know at once she's been christened Cinders for life.

I open my desk drawer, where I swept them last week, and dump the samples out on to my desk.

'Good.' Satisfied, Cindy heads back to her PC.

Ignoring the sample pots, I open a browser window and start searching Facebook. Jeff's profile is easy to find. I check his birthdate. He's Capricorn.

As I crack open a fresh Word doc, Will's voice makes me jump.

'Hi, my name's Will Bold.'

I glance sideways and see him talking on his mobile.

'I'm writing a piece on knife crime for my school webzine.' He leans back in his chair and hooks a leg over the corner of his desk. He sounds so confident and experienced, but then he has won an award for his writing. I sigh and pull my monitor closer, risking eye-burn to stop him seeing what I'm doing.

Will's phone voice is high volume. 'I was wondering if you'd be willing to answer some questions about knife crime in this area.' He scribbles on a notepad and underlines ferociously. I ignore him and start typing.

*Capricorn, Star-ling! Sign of the goat? Never! You don't belong on the farm.*

I grit my teeth as Will bellows into his phone. 'So this year's figures are up on last year?'

*This week, a familiar face will offer you the chance to work with a very unfamiliar flock.*

'And what's the average age of knife-crime victims?' Will's taking notes again.

*Leave your shyness in the barn and polish your horns.*

Will runs his fingers through his hair, frowning. 'So female victims are on the increase? And female offenders? That's interesting.'

I focus on my screen. *Seize this opportunity with both hooves, you lucky goat; it will bring you closer to the opposite sex, and Jessica's not talking about knitting with your nanny.*

I tackle Savannah's horoscope next. It's half-written in my head.

<u>Pisces</u>
*Hey, fish-face!*

OK, so I'm still a little stung from her laughing at my first published article.

*You've been swimming along happily for a while, but watch out. Those goldfish you've been hanging out with may turn out to be sharks. And if there's a curly-haired merman in your life, beware. He may not be flapping his tail just for you.*

Will's phone interview cuts into my train of thought

again. 'Do you have his number?' He makes another note. 'Thanks. You've been a great help.' He ends the call and picks up his notepad. Tapping it with a pen, he frowns.

'Do you need any help?' I switch windows, from my horoscopes back to Facebook, hiding my work.

He narrows his eyes. 'Do you know anything about knife crime?'

'I could do some research for you.' I'm supposed to be editorial assistant for the whole webzine after all, not just product tester for Cindy.

He leans back to get a look at my screen. 'Does Facebook have a page on knife crime then?' he sniffs. 'Perhaps you could become a fan.'

I bristle. 'Facebook is useful for researching *some* things.'

'Yeah, I can see that.' His gaze sweeps the tester pots cluttering my desk then flicks back to his own screen. 'Stick with your face cream. I can handle this.'

*He thinks I'm a ditz!* Furious, I pick up a pot and shake it at him. 'How do you know I'm not writing a piece on animal testing?'

Suddenly the lid frisbees off the pot and a dollop of cream splatters his leather jacket.

*Oh, no! I am a ditz!* My confidence shrivels like a crisp packet in a microwave.

Sam explodes with laughter and drags his earphones out. 'Great aim, Gem!'

Cindy looks up from her desk. 'Oh, dear.' A smile

breaks over her face. 'Rub it in, Will. It might soften you up.'

Eyes blazing, Will pushes back his chair and storms from the room.

'Not bad, Gemma.' Cindy's clearly enjoying my embarrassment. 'You should test some other products on him when he gets back. Maybe wart remover. Banish him for good.' She switches her gaze to Sam, beckoning him over with her pen. 'There's a new band I want you to review.' As Sam leans in, she taps the pen on her screen. 'They're playing Friday night. I thought we could check it out.'

Sam's nodding. 'Great.' He glances at me. 'We could all go. A webzine night out.'

Cindy cuts him off. 'Sorry, Sam.' She lets remorse darken her big blue eyes. 'I've only got two tickets.' She pouts. 'So only enough for you and me, I'm afraid.'

'Oh.' Sam shoves his hands into his pockets. 'OK.' He's so easy-going! No wonder Cindy's got her eye on him. A few more pouts and she'll have him following her round like a happy puppy. Like Barbara. Both of them high on her deadly perfume trail.

I screw the lid back on the pot and pull a tissue from my pocket. Silently fuming, I wipe up the cream dotting my desk. Sometimes it seems as if everybody is having fun except me.

By the next Monday I'm determined that Jeff sees his horoscope asap.

Everyone seems to be starting to believe in Jessica Jupiter's predictions and the column has been getting some very unexpected results. On Thursday mousey Susan Noakes stunned the whole class by declaring that she wanted to sing 'Bad Romance' by Lady Gaga for the Valentine's assembly. When Miss Davis asked her why, Susan stammered that she felt it was really important to present both the positive and negative sides of love. Then she muttered under her breath that the assembly was also a great opportunity to shine.

I don't think anyone else heard her – they were all probably trying to picture Susan tottering round the stage in a pair of platform shoes made from lamb chops. But I remembered my prediction for Virgo about turning shy into shine and realised what had happened. Susan had clearly taken Jessica Jupiter's words to heart. And hopefully, so will Jeff. I need to help Treacle kick-start her love life as soon as possible.

The school bell's rung for the last time and the webzine team have crowded into the storeroom to check issue two before it goes out on Wednesday.

This time Cindy's allocated us one article each. I've been given Barbara's latest stink-piece. I glance nervously at Jeff, wondering what Cindy gave him. Just to be sure he doesn't miss Jessica's personalised prediction, I slide quietly out from behind my desk and sidle across the room.

'Hey, Jeff.' I hold out a copy of this week's predictions. 'Would you mind checking Jessica's column too? She just emailed it over to me and I never know how to spell Pisces.'

Jeff looks up. 'The horoscopes?' He waves his own print-out. 'I'm already checking Phil and Dave's tech piece.'

'It's really short,' I wheedle.

'I can check that if you want, Gemma,' Cindy says. She prickles like a nervous cat whenever someone else takes the initiative.

Will's on to it like a dog on a bone. 'Chill, Cinders. The kid's handling it.' He glances up from his piece on knife crime. It's going to be a two-part series: facts this week, interview next week. I was hoping to proofread it and have an early look, but Will likes to check his own copy. As far as he's concerned, we're not 'real' enough to get it.

I wonder if he'll find his horoscope *real* enough. I remember it word for word.

*Aquarius, you're going to need a bit more than pimple cream to shrink the trouble spots in your life this week. Homework will feel heavy, friends will feel hard work and family will feel irritating. If you want to make it over the bumps, take any help you're offered. If you're too proud to take help, take a hike.*

I thrust Jessica's column harder at Jeff.

'OK then.' He takes it. 'Who are you checking?'

I hold up Barbara's latest masterpiece. *How to Get the Most from Your Homework.*

'Oh.' Jeff reads the title, throwing a weak smile at Barbara.

She's arranging pencils on her desk. She likes to mark spelling mistakes in blue, and grammatical errors in green like a human word-processing app. She looks up and sees us staring at her. 'I hope you're enjoying it, Gemma,' she smiles. 'I really think a little more planning could make homework far more productive and rewarding.'

'Yu-huh.' I sit down and sneak sideways glances at Jeff, relaxing when he switches from the tech piece to the horoscopes. Satisfied, I turn my attention back to Barbara's article and start reading.

*Step One: organise your time*

*The hours between 4.00 pm and 6.00 pm are usually the*

most wasted hours of the day. Set this time aside. Cancel all other arrangements. Make these the most productive hours of your day. If your homework's finished by teatime, you can reward yourself with a full evening of free time for yourself.

*Step Two: organise your workspace*

*Declutter your desk. Turn off your phone. Leave your MP3 player somewhere else. The last thing you need is distractions. The place where you work should be dedicated only to work. Fill a basket with stationery supplies such as pens, pencils, eraser, scissors, highlighters, ruler, calculator, glue, stapler. Then you won't have to run around the house looking for anything and there's no chance you'll get sidetracked.*

I resist a yawn, wishing there was something to sidetrack me right now.

The only Green Park students who are going to read past the first paragraph are probably already organising their time and workspace just fine. The F-class students are just going to flick to Jeff's sports feature or Cindy's beauty column. I sigh. I'm sure my shed idea would set the whole school talking.

I skim to the final paragraph of Barbara's piece.

*Step Seventeen: always, always, always tackle your hardest assignments first*

Yeah, like reading this article before you begin. It'll make your homework seem interesting.

My silent fuming is interrupted by the door swinging

open. It's Miss Bayliss. My gaze sneaks back to Jeff. Has he reached Capricorn yet?

'Jeff,' Miss Bayliss nods at him. 'Mr Chapman said I'd find you here. I wanted a word about the Year Nine girls' football team.'

'Oh.' Jeff looks at her blankly.

'Now they've made it through to the next round of the Cup I think they need to take their skills to a higher level,' Miss Bayliss continues, 'and I was hoping you could find the time to coach them for a few sessions.'

Jeff blinks at her. Then stares down at the page in his hand, eyes popping. I stifle a smile. He's spotted the bait I've planted in the text. Come on, *nibble*! Once he's bitten, he'll be back for more and then Jessica Jupiter can lay a trail of love titbits that will lead him straight into Treacle's arms.

I lean forward as Miss Bayliss raps her fingers on the doorframe.

'So, will you?' she asks.

Jeff glances back at the horoscopes. 'Y-yeah,' he answers uncertainly. 'OK.'

'Great.' Miss Bayliss turns and exits.

Jeff scratches his head. I watch his gaze as it zips over the words once again. His eyebrows are stretched high in disbelief. 'Who *is* this Jessica Jupiter?' He looks up as though he's surprised himself by speaking out loud.

Cindy's tapping away on her keyboard. 'Just some old lady astrologer,' she mutters.

*Old lady? Thanks, Cinders.* I shoot her a death-stare, but she doesn't look up and it sails over her head.

Will's chewing on his pen, watching Jeff thoughtfully. 'What's the matter, Jeff? Has Jupiter told you next week's Cup score?'

Jeff shifts his feet. 'No. It's nothing.' I guess he doesn't want the King of Fact to think he's superstitious.

Grinning, I plough through the last three paragraphs of Barbara's piece. 'No typos,' I report, getting up to swap it for another of the articles stacked on Cindy's desk. As I take a fresh one, Cindy jerks in her seat as though 10,000 volts just passed through it.

'Leave that one!' Cindy barks as she snatches the paper from my hand.

But it's too late. I've already read the headline. *Save Our Shed. Demolition Threatens School Morale.*

She's stolen my idea!

My mouth hangs open as I stare at her. 'Th-that was my idea!' I fumble for words, stunned by her cheek.

'Sam.' Cindy stares straight past me. 'Nice article on Friday's gig. And Will, when you've finished with yours, I'm looking forward to reading it. I think we're really starting to tackle some important issues.' She waltzes from behind her desk and starts collecting in papers. 'Phil and David, great piece on safe Googling.'

I watch her spin around the room like a ballerina gathering props at the end of a performance.

'We should go,' she declares. 'The cleaners will be wanting to get in here.' She's stuffing her backpack with papers and, without even looking in my direction, she scoots past me and heads out the door.

'Wait for me.' Clutching her pencils, Barbara races after her.

I gaze, open-mouthed, as Will, Jeff, David and Phil follow. I just stare after them, Cindy's betrayal stinging like fury. How *dare* she? First she acts like my idea is a piece of junk then she steals it. And I thought *I* was the Evil Genius.

'You OK?'

I spin as I hear Sam's voice. He's zipping his backpack.

'She stole my article.' I can still hardly believe it. But what can I do? Resign? Then I'll never get a chance to write a real story.

'Your bike shed idea?' Sam swings his bag over his shoulder.

'How did she think she'd get away with it?' Blood's roaring in my ears.

Sam pats my shoulder. 'I'm afraid there's not a lot you can do about it.' His blue eyes are round with sympathy. 'Just keep your ideas to yourself in future.'

'Aren't we meant to be a team?'

'Look.' Sam pauses and glances at the floor. 'How about we—'

My phone beeps and I reach for it. Sam waits while I read the text.Mum needs me to pick up Ben's medication before the chemist closes. She's phoned and they're expecting me. The staff there are like a second family.

'I've got to go,' I tell Sam.

'Um, yeah. Me too.' He switches off the light as he follows me out into the corridor. My stomach is cramped with disappointment. Save Our Shed was going to be my breakthrough story. And Cindy stole it.

Silent as squeakless mice, we head along the deserted corridors and push through the front doors, emerging into drizzle. The streetlights are flickering on.

'Bye, Sam.' I hurry for the gate. If I run, I should make it to the chemist before it shuts.

'Bye, Gemma.' Sam's call echoes across the shadowy playground.

# 11

I barge through the front door, happy to be out of the icy wind. It's good to be home. I smell dinner. Something tasty. I drop my schoolbag and hang up my coat. Underneath the mouth-watering food smell is the faint whiff of hospital that always seems to cling to Ben's CF equipment.

'Hi, Dad.' He looks up from his paper as I wander into the living room and drop Ben's prescriptions on the sofa beside him.

'Hi, love.' Dad smiles. 'You look cold. Did you manage to get everything?' He glances at the chemist's bag.

'They only had half the antibiotics, but Mrs MacDonald says we can pick up the other half tomorrow.'

Dad folds his paper. 'Thanks, Gem. Are you hungry?'

'Yeah, I'm starving!' I follow him into the kitchen. 'Where's Ben?'

Dad clatters plates out of the cupboard and lines them up on the counter. 'Mum set his Xbox up in his bedroom.'

'Is he OK?' I'm instantly worried. Mum only lets him play Xbox in bed if he's sick.

'He's fine,' Dad reassures me. 'Just tired. It was his school trip today.'

'Oh, yes! The zoo!' I turn as Mum pads into the kitchen. 'How was it?'

She slides her arms round my waist and hugs me hello. 'It was great.' Mum always volunteers to help out on school trips. That way she can keep an eye on Ben. 'The kids made more noise than the animals.'

'I bet the animals thought you were bringing the zoo to visit them,' I joke.

'The monkeys did look surprised.' Mum lets go of me and leans over to sniff the casserole. Dad's carrying it from the oven. She grabs a cloth and lifts off the lid. Steam billows out, fragrant with onions and herbs.

'Are we eating in front of the telly?' I ask hopefully.

Dad ladles a spoonful of dark, rich casserole on to a plate. 'Why not?'

'Yay!' I grab the plate and carry it through, curling up in my favourite corner of the sofa. 'What about Ben?' I call back into the kitchen.

'Shh!' Mum pokes her head out. 'He's asleep.'

I feel a moment's disappointment, which evaporates as I switch the TV from the cartoon channel and find something with real human beings in it.

'When does the football start?' The sofa heaves as Dad

sits down beside me. I steady my plate as Mum squeezes in next to him.

She raises her eyebrows. 'You think I'm going to watch football after a day at the zoo with seventy-two nine-year-olds?'

'Just the second half?' Dad asks hopefully.

Mum forks in a mouthful of stew. 'OK,' she mumbles. Dad smiles, and I tuck into my dinner.

After we've eaten, I take the plates out and help Dad with the washing-up while Mum has forty winks on the sofa. As Dad wakes her gently with a cup of tea, I hear the doorbell. I race to answer it before it wakes Ben by jangling again. Treacle's standing there, looking as if she's freezing, despite her giant coat.

I hug her and drag her inside. 'What are you doing here?' If there's a match on, she's usually at home, glued to the telly. 'What about the football?'

'I'm recording it.' She points to her schoolbag. 'I'm really struggling with the assignment on *To Kill a Mockingbird* and I know you've read it.'

'Haven't you?'

'Two-thirds,' she admits.

I close the front door quietly. 'That'll be enough to write the assignment,' I tell her. 'It's just a character study.'

I lean into the living room, swinging on the door handle. 'Treacle's here. We're going to do homework.'

Mum and Dad are already snuggled up in the middle of the sofa. Mum looks up sleepily. 'OK, Gem. Do you want ice cream or anything?'

'We can get some later if we do.' I pull the door to and lead Treacle upstairs. I can't resist checking on Ben. He's fast sleep, his mouth just wide enough to make tiny snores.

'He's so cute,' Treacle whispers behind me.

'Don't let him hear you say that!' I warn her. 'He'll kill you.'

She grins and heads for my room. In five minutes we've got papers spread over the floor and our copies of the book cracked open and face down.

'You'll never believe what Cindy did.' It's the first chance I've had to dish the dirt on the Ice Queen's latest crime and I'm relieved Treacle's here so I can dirt-dish in person.

'What?' Treacle's eyes are wide.

'She stole the article.'

'The article?'

'The shed article,' I prompt.

'The *SHED* article?'

The shock in her voice pleases me. It convinces me I'm right to be furious.

'You know I mentioned it to her last week and she brushed me off like it was a dumb idea?' I remind her. Treacle nods as I go on. 'Well, she's written her own version and she's publishing it in next week's webzine.'

Treacle shakes her head. 'She's unbelievable!'

'I know!'

'Did you say anything to her?'

'She didn't give me a chance,' I splutter. 'She just ended the meeting and left.'

'What are you going to do about it?' Treacle asks.

'What *can* I do?' I sigh.

'We could make a voodoo doll of her and stick pins in it,' Treacle suggests.

I let out a sigh. 'A voodoo doll won't make me feature writer on the webzine.'

Treacle picks up her bag from the floor beside her. 'Let's forget about her then.'

I reach for my book. 'Shall we do the essay?'

Treacle shakes her head then starts fumbling in her bag. 'I want you to hear something. It's for the Valentine's assembly.' She pulls out a book and I notice that her face has gone bright red. 'It's a poem.'

I shudder. Because Susan decided that she wanted to sing in the assembly, Miss Davis has decided that the rest of us should contribute 'creatively' too and read famous love poems to the rest of the school. She thinks St Valentine will be pleased.

I'm not. I'm mortified. 'I can't believe she wants us to read such soppy stuff out loud. To *everyone*.'

'Yeah well, I've found one I kind of like.' Treacle's face is so red now I can practically feel the heat radiating off it.

I lean over and read upside down.

'Valentine' by Carol Ann Duffy.

I've never heard of it. I've not chosen my poem yet. I'm having a hard enough time practising the intro Miss Davis has given me to read. *Valentine's Day is a day to celebrate love and love is one of the strongest forces in the universe.* Hmm, not quite as strong as the force of embarrassment I'm going to feel reading it to the rest of the school.

Treacle is on her feet and shaking back her hair. She holds up the book and starts reading.

'"Valentine" by Carol Ann Duffy.' She coughs, goes a bit redder, then continues.

'Not a red rose or a satin heart.
I give you an onion.'

I do a double-take. 'An onion?'

'Wait.' Treacle holds up a hand. 'It gets better.' She lifts the book until it is completely covering her blushing face.

'It is a moon wrapped in brown paper.
It promises light

like the careful undressing of love.
Here.
It will blind you with tears
like a lover.'

'Wow.' I'm liking it.

'Is it OK?' Treacle lets the book droop and stares at me. 'Perhaps I should choose something soppier.'

'Since when was *real* love actually soppy?' I point out. 'Look at Savannah. Her love life seems to consist of arranging dates and making phone calls. It's more like being a secretary.'

Treacle's eyes go misty. 'I'd be a secretary if it meant going out with Jeff. Not that it's ever going to happen.' She shoots a look at me that takes me by surprise. It's sharp with accusation. 'You spend so much time talking to him these days, he'll probably ask you out first.'

'No way!' I react fiercely. 'He's a really nice guy and—'

'So you *do* like him?' Treacle starts picking at the spine of her book.

'Not like *that*!' I say quickly. 'I mean as a friend.'

'Well, you did look pretty *friend*ly at the Cup match,' she mutters.

I sit back in shock. How long has Treacle been feeling like this? 'I was helping him with his report,' I begin.

Then I remember my heart-covered match stats. 'Well, not exactly helping, just . . .'

Treacle wraps her arms round her knees and scowls. 'Just laughing and flirting by the look of it,' she snaps.

'I was not flirting!' I defend myself. 'He's a nice guy. He's easy to be with.'

Treacle starts shoving her books into her bag. 'Yeah, well, I wouldn't know, would I?'

'Treacle!' I grab her arm, but she shakes me off.

'I thought you were trying to help me, but maybe you're after him for yourself.' She stands up and I duck out of the way as she swings her backpack over her shoulder.

'Treacle! I *am* trying to help you. Honestly, you have no idea quite how hard I am trying.'

Treacle drops her bag back on to the floor. 'What do you mean?'

I sigh. I hadn't wanted to tell Treacle about my cunning plan until I knew for sure that it was going to work, but if I want to stop her from walking out in a huff, it looks like I have no choice. 'Well, you know how I'm using Savannah's horoscope to tell her about Josh two-timing?'

Treacle nods.

'I'm doing the same thing for you and Jeff.'

Treacle stares at me like I'm a crazy person. 'What do you mean?'

'I'm going to make him believe in his horoscope and then I'm going to use it to lead him to you.' I sit back, grinning at her broadly, and praying that she loves it and doesn't think I'm insane.

'But how will you get him to believe in it? He's a boy. Boys hate astrology.' Despite Treacle's frown she sits back down next to me. I breathe a sigh of relief.

'I found something out about him the other day, something even he didn't know, and I put it in his horoscope. Then I got him to read it at the meeting today and guess what?'

Treacle looks at me blankly. 'What?'

'It came true almost straight away!'

'What came true?'

I struggle to contain my glee. 'He's going to be coaching the Year Nine girls' football team. *Your* football team.'

'What? Really?' Treacle's face lights up like a Christmas tree.

I nod. 'Yep. And now he thinks Jessica Jupiter is the bee's knees because she predicted it would happen. Hopefully, he'll believe anything she says from now on.'

Treacle shakes her head and for a split second I think she's going to tell me that I'm nuts and my plan stinks. But then she starts to grin. 'I'm so sorry, Gem. I don't know why I ever thought you liked him. I've been going crazy thinking I'd never get to talk to him properly. And thinking of you getting to see him on the webzine all the time felt horrible. But he's really going to be coaching the girls' team?'

I nod. 'So you're going to have loads of opportunities to talk to him. *And* you'll have Jessica Jupiter helping out behind the scenes.'

Treacle starts to laugh and her giggle is infectious. 'Think of the power you could have if everyone started to believe in the horoscopes.'

I give an evil cackle. 'World domination will be mine!'

We both crack up laughing. Then Treacle grabs her can of Coke from my bedside table.

'To Jessica Jupiter!' she says, raising the can.

'To Jessica Jupiter!' I say with a grin.

# 12

Icy drizzle is streaming down the windows. The classroom smells of steaming duffle coats and wet hair gel. I glance at the clock. Five minutes until registration. The door's swinging open and shut like it's happy hour at Pizza Hut as damp kids stumble in from the cold. Susan bursts in with her iPod clamped to her ears. She is wearing a rain cape that looks like it has been made out of a bin liner decorated with silver foil patches. I had no idea what I might unleash with Jessica's horoscopes! I cling to the radiator, trying to thaw out, while Treacle paces in front of me.

'I *tackled* him!' She flings her arms wide. 'I tackled Jeff Simpson and won the ball.' She stops and stares at me, as happy as Cinderella the morning after the ball. 'I still can't believe he's coaching our team. He says he's going to give me some one-on-one training to help me with my dribbling.'

'It's your drooling you need help with,' I tease.

Treacle thumps me, then widens her eyes like a soap

star overacting. 'Hey, I forgot. The webzine's out today. Have you seen it yet?'

I nod, clenching my teeth.

Treacle frowns. 'Cindy's shed article?'

'Top story.'

'That is *beyond* unfair.'

As she speaks, Savannah sweeps in. Her head's bowed. She's reading a print-out. 'I don't see how Jessica Jupiter can be so right one week and so wrong another.' She flops on to the desk next to me and pokes her paper with a polished fingernail. '*And if there's a curly-haired merman in your life, beware. He may not be flapping his tail just for you,*' she quotes. 'The only curly-haired man in my life is Josh.' Her brow furrows. 'Is she saying that he's seeing someone else?'

'Who knows?' I answer innocently.

'She's an idiot.' Savannah flicks her hair back. 'Where is Josh anyway?' She scans the class.

I shrug. He's usually here by now, but there's no sign of him. I check to see if Chelsea's missing too. But she's skulking by the window, one eye on the door.

Savannah sighs. 'He must have missed his bus.' She screws up the print-out.

'Hey, are those Jessica's horoscopes?' Chelsea points at the balled paper. 'Can I read them?'

'Sure.' Savannah flings the paper at Chelsea.

'Thanks.'

I nibble on a nail as Chelsea smoothes out the paper and starts reading. I hope she doesn't pick up my zodiacal warning. I don't want her taking evasive action. What's the point in raising Savannah's suspicions if Chelsea backs off till the heat's off? Savannah needs to find out what's going on.

Treacle's furiously trying to catch my eye, but I can't look at Treacle *and* keep up the innocent act with Savannah. I flash Treacle 'Back Off' signals, and am relieved when Miss Davis comes in.

'OK, class.' Her tone tells me she's in super-efficient mode. 'Quick registration. I want to run through our assembly before first lesson. Susan, have you brought your music?'

Susan nods and waves her iPod enthusiastically. I notice that she's painted one nail on each hand bright blue.

'Good.' Miss Davis looks at the rest of the class. 'Have you all brought your poems?' As she ticks off names, we rummage for our books and print-outs.

'I've left mine in my locker,' Marcus mumbles.

Miss Davis looks up, sucking the end of her pen. 'You're Byron, aren't you?'

Ryan laughs. 'More like *mo*ron.'

Miss Davis ignores him. She's searching through the pile of books on her table. She pulls one out. 'She walks in beauty, like the night.' She passes him the book. 'Page 204, I think.'

I grab my rucksack, warm from the radiator, and pull out the sheet I've printed from the internet. I found a poem I like at last. Emily Dickinson.

I hide myself within my flower,
That wearing on your breast,
You, unsuspecting, wear me too—
And angels know the rest.

It seemed an appropriate poem for an undercover Cupid.

Miss Davis calls Marcus to the front of the class. 'Why don't you start us off.'

Marcus is blushing as he flicks through the book and begins reading.

'She walks in beauty like the night, of cloudless climes and starry skies . . .' His eyes are fixed firmly on the page, face down, neck red as a raspberry.

'Look *up*!' Miss Davis encourages. 'The audience are going to want to see your face.'

Chelsea coughs. 'Are you sure, Miss?'

'Humiliation' should be top of the list, right next to 'Throwing Kids in Front of Buses' as Number One No-No for teachers. My heart aches for Marcus, but Miss Davis seems oblivious to his agony.

He ducks closer to his page, his voice a monotone. 'And all that's best of dark and bright.' His gaze flicks towards Savannah, then back to the page. 'Meet in her aspect and her eyes—'

Suddenly the door flies open and Chelsea looks up like a dog hearing the rattle of a biscuit barrel.

Josh arrives, panting. 'Sorry I'm late, Miss. Bus was late.' He slides behind a desk. Savannah peels away from us and takes the seat beside him.

Chelsea's watching from the next desk. I see her mouth curve into a smile as she rips a corner from her jotter and scribbles something on it.

Savannah's whispering in Josh's ear, but he shrugs her away, looking for something in his rucksack. Savannah scowls and slouches sulkily in her chair. She starts flicking through her poetry book.

And then it happens.

Chelsea makes her move.

I clutch Treacle's arm as Chelsea reaches out and flaps a note beside Josh's knee. He zips his bag shut, leans down to stow it against the desk leg and takes the note from Chelsea.

My gaze flits to Savannah. Is she still buried in her book?

No.

She's staring at the small piece of white paper in Josh's hand. She snatches it from him and reads it. 'No way!'

'Thus mellowed to that tender light—' Marcus continues reading, but Savannah's yelp of horror stops him mid-sentence. The class's attention swivels towards her.

'What's the matter now?' Miss Davis sighs.

'Meet me behind the bike shed after school?' Savannah's reading the note out loud. She glares at Chelsea, her eyes blazing. Chelsea smiles, long and slow. Savannah's rage fixes on Josh. 'How could you?'

The whole class is enthralled. Then I notice Marcus. His eyes are round, like a dove's. There's no satisfaction there, only sympathy as he gazes at Savannah.

Savannah hasn't finished. 'And with *her*?' She points at Chelsea. I can see Savannah's eyes brimming with tears. Guilt surges through me.

*It's not your fault,* I tell myself. It's Josh who's been two-timing and Chelsea who passed the note. I just tried to give Savannah an early warning.

Savannah blinks, her eyes clearing. 'I thought you liked me, but clearly you prefer fish that are easy to catch.' She throws Chelsea a withering glance. 'We're finished, Mr Merman!'

Josh gapes at her. 'What?'

'Jessica Jupiter was right!' Savannah tosses back her hair. 'If you want to flap your tail at Chelsea, go ahead. You can swim away into the ocean and drown for all I care!'

'Go, Savannah!' Sally shouts, punching the air.

The class break into a spontaneous cheer. Treacle's

135

whooping beside me. I feel a flood of pride. *Well done, Savannah!*

'Now, now, class!' As Miss Davis flaps like a dodo making one last attempt at flight, Savannah hunches down in her seat. I want to give her a hug. She looks like she could use one, and when the bell goes, I manage to catch her before we split up for the next lesson.

'I'm sorry, Savannah,' I sympathise.

Treacle bobs in beside us. 'It's better you found out now.'

Savannah's half hiding behind her hair. She doesn't look angry any more, just really, really sad. 'It's so embarrassing,' she mutters.

'Only for him.' I throw Josh a death-stare. He's exiting the classroom with the rest of the class, steering clear of Chelsea who's eyeing him like a hopeful puppy. Red-faced, he slides into a gaggle of boys and glances ruefully back at Savannah.

Savannah shakes her head. 'But *Chelsea*?'

'He clearly doesn't have good taste.' Treacle raises her voice loud enough for Chelsea to hear.

'We'll talk about it at lunchtime, OK?' I give Savannah a quick hug. She's got German; we've got Spanish.

'Yeah.' She heads away down the hall. 'Thanks.'

I glance at Treacle. 'I hope she's OK.'

'We'll cheer her up,' Treacle promises.

136

'Savannah!'

I hail her across the lunch hall, bobbing and weaving through the crowds to her table, trailing Treacle in my wake.

Savannah is looking surprisingly OK. Sal and Anila are clustered at her table with Marcus.

Laughing, Anila snatches a piece of paper from Sal and starts reading out loud. 'Aries.' As she reads on, I recognise Jessica's words.

*'Star-ling, I have wonderful news. This week may seem to be littered with nothing but empty bubblegum wrappers . . .'*

(I'd been staring at the overflowing wastepaper basket in the webzine HQ.)

*'. . . but don't despair. On Friday a surprise lollipop will add a little sugar to your life.'*

(Guess what I was sucking as I typed?)

*'It may not satisfy you, but it'll keep you going until Saturday when a shopping trip turns out to be sweeter than you think. Just make sure you have your toothbrush handy or you might find a little plaque with your name on it.'*

Sal's clapping her hands like an overexcited seal. 'This woman's a genius!'

Savannah's nodding. 'How did she know Josh was sneaking around with Chelsea?'

On the other side of the lunch hall some shouting breaks out. A Year Eight girl is waving a piece of paper in front of an embarrassed-looking boy sitting next to her, who I assume must be her boyfriend. 'Well, you must have done something,' the girl shouts. 'Jessica doesn't lie.'

Her boyfriend runs his hand through his hair. His curly hair. Oh, dear. I hunch over my sandwiches and don't dare look at Treacle.

'Listen to this!' Anila's reading again. '*Wednesday morning will bring a nasty surprise.*'

(Will had walked into the room while I was typing and made me jump.)

'OMG!' Sal claps her hand over her mouth. 'She knew about the German test!'

Anila slaps the paper down on the table. 'She's psychic. No question.'

I lift my lunch box to cover my smile. If only they knew how random my predictions were!

✩ ✩ ✩

'I don't know about you . . .' Cindy pauses and gazes dramatically around the storeroom. '. . . but I don't think there's *anything* here fit for publication.' She drops a thick wad of papers into the bin beside her desk.

We're reviewing the article submissions sent in by our readers.

I stare at the bin and grind my teeth. I know what it's like to be cold-shouldered by the Ice Queen. She'll probably be picking through the submissions later, looking

for something to steal. I imagine her like a bag lady –
fingerless gloves, skewed hat, scuffed boots – crouched
over the bin, chuckling as she snatches at the discarded
papers and scours them for inspiration.

Will's leather jacket creaks as he shifts in his seat. 'For
once, we agree.'

Sam looks out from under his hair. 'The article on
improving school dinners was OK,' he ventures.

Will snorts. 'Who eats school dinners?'

'We do,' Phil pipes up.

David nods. 'They're really not that bad.'

Will holds up his hands. 'Well, in that case they don't
need improving.'

Barbara moves to the edge of her seat eagerly. 'Well
hopefully, my suggestion for next week's lifestyle feature
will cheer you all up.'

'Quick, tell us.' Will leans forward, chin on hands,
eyes wide. 'The suspense is giving me an ulcer.'

Jeff kicks Will's leg. 'Cut the sarcasm, Will.'

But Barbara's completely immune to his jibes. She's as
comfortable with her dull ideas as she is with her sensible shoes. I silently envy her thick skin as she makes her
announcement.

'How to be the Perfect Prefect.'

Will clutches his chest. 'You're killing me.'

Cindy raises an eyebrow. 'I think it's a fine idea.'

I fidget in my seat. It's not a fine idea. It's as dull as

every other Barbara-special. I've got to speak up. I'll regret it later if I don't. 'Could I have a go at writing an article?' The air suddenly feels syrupy-thick.

Will puts an arm over the back of his chair and stretches out. 'Fourteen Fab Facebook Groups?'

I silently shower him with high-expletive thought-bombs.

Cindy smiles at me like a nursery school teacher admiring a pasta collage. 'Why don't we talk about it later, Gemma?' She turns to the others, pushing back her shoulders like she means business. 'I've already planned my next article.'

She's dismissed me *again*! I swallow back rage.

Will lolls in his chair. 'Go ahead, Cinders. I don't know if anything can top Barbara's prefect piece, but it's worth a try.'

Cindy narrows her eyes. 'My article next week,' she announces, 'will be "Make Every Day a Great Hair Day".'

Will drops his head into his hands with a groan. 'I wish you'd warned me I'd be writing for *Teengirl*.'

Cindy doesn't flinch. 'I wish you'd warned me you were so arrogant.'

Sam shifts his chair forward. 'Look,' he says like a peace envoy attempting to stop the outbreak of World War Three, 'we're bound to have different ideas about the webzine, but I really think there's room for different voices.'

Phil's nodding. 'We *are* trying to cater to a diverse readership.'

While Sam and Phil broker a peace deal, I'm fighting bitterness. 'Why isn't there room for me to write an article then?' I ask.

Sam opens his mouth, but Cindy butts in. 'I *said* we'd talk about that later, Gemma.' She's on her feet and swinging her backpack over her shoulder. I can't believe she's signalling the meeting's over.

I look around, hoping someone will want to stay and talk more, but Will's zipping his bag and the twins are heading for the door. Sam gives me a sympathetic shrug and stands up.

The Ice Queen has silenced me *again*, but this time she's not making the fastest exit. She leans over her desk and starts fiddling with papers until the others leave.

'Wait outside,' she chirrups to Barbara. 'I won't be a moment.'

As soon as we're alone, she drops her pretty voice. And her sweeter-than-thou act. 'Look,' she hisses, 'Jessica Jupiter is doing great. She's even getting fan mail.'

'Fan mail?' I stare at her.

'It's OK,' she tells me. 'I'm going to set up an email account in her name and you can check it and reply to everyone.'

'Thanks,' I growl.

'As it's going so well, I need you to keep concentrating on the horoscopes.' She switches off her monitor. 'I don't want you getting distracted by silly articles.'

'Like the one you stole off me?' I challenge.

'You gave me an idea, I ran with it,' she snaps. 'I think you'll find that anyone can have ideas, but only *some* of us have the commitment to follow them through.'

Before I can answer, she sashays from the room. 'Come on, Barbie, let's go home.' Her voice echoes in the corridor outside. 'Switch the lights off, Gem sweetie.'

I don't know whether to laugh or cry. My column's a success. I'm getting fan mail. But the horoscopes weren't meant to be my greatest moment. They were meant to be stepping stone to something better.

Still fuming, I head down to the football field. The Year Nine girls' team are making the most of the fading light to get in extra practice for the semi-final tomorrow. I wave at Treacle, who's jogging on the spot, trying to keep warm in the icy wind while she waits for her turn to practise penalties. We can get the bus home together.

Jeff's on the sideline, watching.

I stop beside him. 'How are they doing?' I ask as I clap my arms to try and keep warm.

He nods thoughtfully as Jing-Wei lands a penalty kick in the back of the goal. He's clearly taking his job as extra coach seriously. 'If they keep practising, they should be OK.'

'Do you think they can win the Cup?'

'There are some strong players,' he answers. 'Treacle's great on goal and Anila's a useful winger. If we can just make the defence stronger, I think they could win.'

I let the Treacle comment pass unhyped. From now on I'm letting Jessica fire the Cupid arrows. Instead, I opt for sport-talk. 'Treacle says that if they win the Cup, they go on to the regionals.'

'Yep.' Jeff stuffs his wind-chilled hands into his pockets. 'But the regionals are a whole different ball game.'

'Really?' I look at him innocently. 'Do they switch to rugby?'

He glances at me then rolls his eyes as he realises I'm joking. 'I'm serious. They'll have to add additional training, like swimming or running, to build up their stamina.'

'Is that what you do?' I know Jeff plays football for the county as well as the school.

'I run every morning before school.'

*So does Treacle!* I bite my tongue before I blurt it out. 'Don't you get tired from all that exercise?'

'Nah. Your body gets used to it.' His breath billows in the wind. 'And it's not like I'm exercising all the time. I still do fun stuff like go to the movies.'

'You like movies?' I take out my mental notebook. I'm fact-gathering for Jessica Jupiter. 'What kind?'

He shrugs. 'Comedy mostly.'

Football. Running. Funny films! The more I learn about Jeff, the more he seems to be the boy-version of Treacle. I suddenly remember his Comic-Con comment at last week's meeting. It's a lead that needs following up. 'Did you say you went to last year's Comic-Con too?' I try to sound casual. With any luck, he'll just assume I'm chattering away because I'm a girl.

'How'd you know?' He snaps his head round.

'You told the twins at the meeting.' I shrug carelessly. 'You said you got Dave Gibbons's autograph.'

'Oh, yeah,' he remembers and hunches deeper into his jacket. 'I'm a total comic book geek.' He sounds apologetic.

I want to squeal, *So is Treacle!*

But I don't. Instead, I cover my mouth to hide my smile as he goes on.

'Working with Phil and Dave on the webzine is pretty cool,' he confesses. 'They know everything there is to know about the Green Goblin.'

I nod wisely. 'Spiderman's enemy.'

He steps back. 'How'd you know that?'

'Treacle.' I hold my hands up. 'When that girl says she's got issues, she means back issues. About two hundred of them stacked inside her wardrobe. Her dad started her on Superman when she was a kid and now she's completely hooked.'

'Her dad should meet mine.' Jeff grins. 'Together they might be able to finally decide whether *Omega the Unknown* or *Sword of the Atom* is the most underrated comic book of all time.'

I look at him blankly. 'I'm afraid my only experience of a comic book is the *Beano* annual.'

'Watch out,' Jeff warns. 'It always starts out with a few Dennis the Menace strips and then, before you know it, you're on the hard stuff. I need at least three *Aquamans* to get to sleep at night.'

We're laughing so hard I don't see Treacle arrive. She's standing at my elbow, kitbag swinging, frowning. 'Are you ready to go, Gemma?'

'Sure. We were just talking about—' but Treacle has already turned and started stomping off towards the gate. I shrug and smile at Jeff. 'See you at Friday's meeting then.' I race off after Treacle. 'Hey, wait for me.' I tug on her coat sleeve as I catch her up. 'Why didn't you say hi to Jeff?'

'It looked like you had the conversation under control.' Treacle's marching like there's an oompah band at our heels.

'Slow down!' The freezing air's scorching my lungs as I struggle to keep up.

'No!' she shoots back, her gaze fixed ahead.

Oh, no! Surely she isn't jealous again? But her next snapping comment confirms it.

'How's Jeff ever supposed to notice *me* with you dancing in front of him like a Barbie doll in a blender?'

'Treacle!' I'm running after her as she strides through the gates and sets off towards the bus stop. She's flagging down the bus like an angry granny by the time I catch up.

I leap on to the bus and follow her to a seat at the back. 'We've been through all this. I'm trying to help you. We were talking about comic books!'

She crosses her arms and frowns at me. 'Why were you talking about comic books? You hate comic books.'

'Exactly!' I exclaim. 'So why would Jeff be interested in me when he has more in common with you than I do?'

Treacle blinks. 'Does he?'

'He runs every morning.' I tug her sleeve excitedly. 'Hey! Brainwave! We could find out his route – maybe you could steer your run his way.' I realise I'm veering off topic. 'And he likes funny movies and comic books. That's why we were talking about them. I was finding out info for you!'

'Oh.' Treacle's smiling now. 'Sorry, Gem. I'm just so nervous about tomorrow's semi-final. I'm not thinking straight.'

The bus sways round a corner and I grab the seat to stop from sliding. 'You two are perfect for each other.' I look at her, serious. 'I'd never go for Jeff.' I drop my bag between my feet. It's weighed down with homework. 'Anyway, I don't have time to think about boys,' I tell her. 'Let alone *like* one.'

☆ ☆ ☆

When I get home, the quietness in the house unnerves me. Mum's usually banging plates in or out of the dishwasher, or thumping the vac round or shooting aliens on the Xbox with Ben (she's the slowest space cop in the universe but Ben's very patient with her).

But today the house is silent.

'Mum?' I call uncertainly, shoving my bag beside the radiator. As I hang up my coat, Mum appears from the living room.

'Shh.' She ruffles my hair softly. 'Ben's sleeping.'

Now I'm really concerned. Mum only ruffles my hair when one of us is worried. And Ben is always wide awake when I get home from school.

*Except . . .*

'Another school trip?' I ask hopefully. Mum shakes her head.

'Has he got an infection?' I ask, heart dropping. Mum nods.

Chest infections are like alligators under the bed in our house. Except you can't keep them away just by checking.

Mum looks tired. She's probably been looking after Ben all day without a break.

'I'll do his physio tonight,' I offer.

She rubs her forehead distractedly. 'But he's grumpy when he's got a bug,' she reminds me.

'I'll cheer him up,' I promise brightly.

I have to fall off the tilt-table twice to make him laugh, but it's worth it. Mum's lying down, Dad's cooking supper. Ben's lying on his table looking pale. His nebulizer made him throw up earlier, but he's giggling now. Just about. I want to grab him and hold him close, as if hugging him can keep the germs away from his fragile lungs. But hugging won't help; it'll only let him know I'm scared.

I can hear Dad singing downstairs. He's grilling burgers.

Has Ben learnt to spot the brittle happiness we fake whenever he's ill? I wonder if he feels the shift in gravity as our universe tightens around him.

'Ready?' I haul myself to my feet and roll up my sleeves for the pummelling.

Ben shifts on the table. 'Yep.' His breath is shallow, as though moving is an effort.

I start gently thumping his chest. He feels warm. He must be running a fever.

I carry on, my mind drifting with the rhythm of the pummelling. Then I have an idea. I could write an article about this; what family life is like when someone has a serious medical condition. No one knows how I live; what I think or feel when it comes to Ben. They don't know that I actually don't care whether every day's a Great Hair Day. I complain about my dumb curls but I know, deep down, that straight hair doesn't really matter.

It suddenly feels important to share. Important for me

and important for the webzine's readers. We're all trying to appear so perfect, but life's not perfect – *we're* not perfect – and the best Hair Day in the world won't change anything that's truly important.

But how will I ever persuade Cindy to publish a serious article when she knocks back my ideas like a Wimbledon champ swatting tennis balls?

The next morning Ben's infection hasn't got any better. But it hasn't got any worse, so Mum tells me not to worry and sends me off to school. Before I go I make her promise about fifty times that she'll text me if there's any change.

When Treacle and I get to school, we pass a couple of Year Ten boys who are huddled by the gate, deep in conversation.

'It's Jessica Jupiter,' I hear one of them say and I freeze. How does he know I'm Jessica?

'Apparently, she said that Taureans have to play the field or something, so Michelle told me she can't see me any more.'

I breathe a sigh of relief. They don't know it's me. Then I think back to my horoscope for Taurus: *Time to stop being a bull in a china shop and start playing the field*. I had been thinking about the school playing fields and Jeff coaching Treacle at the time.

'Well, she told my sister that she needed to take up knitting! Now, rather than buying me a birthday present, she's planning to make me something "special and unique" to wear to my party. It's going to be awful, I know it!' the other boy says with a look of horror on his face. I do a quick mental scan of this week's horoscopes and realise his sister must be a Gemini. *A stitch in time will save ninety-nine*, I had written, while trying to think of a Jessica-style saying and hearing the chimes of the ice-cream van outside the school.

'Why do girls believe in all that stuff?' the first boy asks.

'Cos they're dumb,' the second one replies. 'Wanna game of crab football?'

'Sure.'

After they've gone, Treacle looks at me and grins. 'Looks like Jessica has a lot to answer for!'

I link arms with her and we make our way across the rain-slicked playground. 'Well, as long as a certain Year Ten football coach believes what she says, that's all that matters.'

☆ ☆ ☆

The day passes slower than a tortoise with arthritis. Treacle and I are both a bundle of nerves – me about Ben and her about the afternoon's semi-final. Just before the end of last period I get a text from Mum.

*Ben's temp almost back to normal* ☺ *Have fun at the football!* x

'It's a lucky omen,' I say to Treacle as I show her the text. 'Ben is getting better and you're going to win.'

Treacle gives me a nervous smile. 'I hope so. Great news about Ben though.'

When the bell rings, Treacle races off to the PE Department to get changed and I head to the webzine HQ. The match isn't starting for another half an hour and I need to get this week's horoscopes finished.

I'm relieved to find the HQ empty. I sit down at Will's PC, finally able to bag the fastest processor. I've hardly time to unpack my jotter before it's asking me for my login.

I open my Inbox and blink in surprise. Cindy has sent me an email with the login details for Jessica Jupiter's new email address. I login, surprised to see the amount of mail in there already. Excited, I open the first mail.

Dear Jessica,
I love your horroscopes. How do you know so mutch? Are you really physic? Who's going to win the match this afternoon?
luv
Michelle

I sit back and drum my nails on the desk. I've not bitten them in two weeks and they're already long enough to click against the Formica. Jessica's voice echoes in my head and I start typing.

Dearest Michelle,

How sweet of you to write. Next time you might want to use Spellcheck.

The match result is uncertain. Like choosing what to wear for the red carpet, the stars simply can't decide. But I sense that a star-performer on Green Park High's team will outshine the opposition.

Yours star-gazingly,

Jessica

I click Send and open the next message.

Dear Jessica,

Last week you said I was going to have a trip. I fell down the stairs. How did you know?

Cheers

Kevin

I grin as I type.

Dearest Kevin,

What a tragedy! I hope you were not badly hurt. But I did warn you. Ignore Jessica at your peril. Save your next trip for Summer rather than Fall.

Best wishes for a speedy recovery,

Jessica

Enough fan mail. I look at my watch. Fifteen minutes till kick-off. There's still time to write a few horoscopes. I'll start with Jeff's.

In a blank document, I start typing.

## Capricorn

*You've had a busy week, Star-ling. Jessica knows from experience that sharing your gifts with others is tiring. But you will be rewarded. The stars sing of victory, both in sport and in love. The number ten holds the key to your happiness. Look out for it, because it's the one number you can count on this week.*

Only an idiot would miss a hint like that. Ten is the number on the back of Treacle's football shirt. A nervous flutter hits my stomach. Will Treacle think I'm being too obvious?

I shrug. Jeff's a boy. He's not going to overanalyse. He probably won't even *analyse.*

I start work on Savannah's horoscope. She needs cheering up. That's obvious from the extra make-up she's been wearing. Josh's low blow has knocked her confidence.

## Pisces

*Star-ling, last week may have felt like a disaster. But whether it was love, work or family that let you down, you made the right choice. Now the way ahead is clear. Swim forward happily, dear Pisces. The stars are gazing down kindly upon you this week. And treat yourself to something special. You deserve it.*

I hit Return and keep typing. Cindy's not going to get such an easy ride.

*Scorpio*

*With such a nasty sting in your tail, you'd better move with care. You're more poisonous than you think. Try to be gentler with those around you, particulary those younger than you. They lack your barbed backside and can't sting back.*

I stare at the words on the screen. Although it made me feel a whole lot better typing them, Cindy will hate it and then she'll make my life at the webzine even more miserable. I pause, then delete, then start typing again.

*Scorpio*

*A fresh idea will come from an unexpected source. Treat it sweetly. You're smart enough to know that honey works far better than poison.*

I know Cindy won't take Jessica's advice; not when she knows *I'm* Jessica. But I've worded it tactfully. Perhaps my words can slip beneath the ice shield.

I imagine Cindy back on her perfect pink bedspread, proofing my column. Her gaze drifts thoughtfully over Scorpio – she's reading, she's smiling, she's dialling Barbara. 'You know, Barbara,' – her gaze turns thoughtful – 'I think I've underestimated Gemma Stone.'

*Stop dreaming!* I look at my watch. Five minutes left. I can cram in a last paragraph.

_Libra_

My sign. And Mum's. I know I can't actually make the stars do what I want, but there's no harm in hoping.

_You may feel the scales haven't tipped in your favour this week. But don't fret, Star-ling. Good fortune will be linked to a young man with a three-letter name._

Ben.

I send a silent prayer to the stars as I power down the PC. _Please let him get better soon._

I jump as the door squeaks open.

It's Will. He scowls at me as he wanders in. 'That's my PC.'

I meet his gaze steadily. 'The computers belong to everyone.'

He grunts, eyeing the desk suspiciously. 'I hope you haven't messed with anything.'

'I've been too busy with my own work to bother with yours,' I tell him.

He reaches across the desk. I lean out of the way as he jerks open the drawer beside me and pulls out some papers. He opens his bag, shoves the papers into it, then fishes out his mobile phone.

'Still no calls.' He says, sounding disappointed.

'Expecting one?'

'I was trying to set up an interview with a knife-crime victim.'

I want to offer help again. Someone who's been

stabbed might respond better to a fourteen-year-old girl than a surly fifteen-year-old boy. But I don't say anything. *If you're too proud to take help, take a hike.* I remember his horoscope. I doubt he's even read it.

'Shame.' I grab my bag and head for the match. I'm not going to give him another chance to point out what a hopeless ditz I am.

✪ ✪ ✪

I arrive panting at the sideline just as the ref blows his whistle for the kick-off. A thin crowd is dotted round the edge of the pitch. Eager parents watch in clusters.

The Green Park team spread out, battle-ready from the off. Treacle nods at me from centrefield and then launches herself at the ball.

'Hi.' I jump as I hear Jeff's voice behind me. I turn and see him walking towards me holding a notebook.

I blink in surprise. I hadn't even noticed him. 'Hi. Are you taking notes for the webzine?'

'Yep.' He narrows his eyes as Treacle makes a charge for goal, and groans as she's tackled away.

'If you need me to add any hearts or flowers, just ask,' I joke.

He grins. 'Nah, I think I'll be fine without, thanks.'

Treacle is playing brilliantly. She hooks the ball from between a winger's feet and makes a break, crossing to Jing-Wei who heads a long ball over the bar.

Jeff gets so caught up in the action he stops note-taking. 'I didn't know girls could play football like this.' He sounds genuinely impressed.

It's an all-out battle on pitch – good-humoured – but both sides are playing like their lives depend on it.

Anila punches away a ball as the opposing team, Westbury High, make an attack on our goal. Green Park are struggling to get possession; Westbury High keep pushing us back. Then Erin Slater steals the ball and zig-zags down the pitch, dribbling her way past both defenders and striking a powerful kick into the side netting just as the ref blows the half-time whistle.

'Wow! It's a really exciting game!' I say, turning to Jeff, but he's busy scribbling notes in his jotter.

When the second half begins, Karen sends a low drive wide.

'Come on!' Jeff urges. 'Score!' He gives a heartfelt groan as Treacle flashes an effort across the face of the goal, missing by a whisker.

My heart starts to race as Westbury High punt the ball back upfield, veering dangerously close to our goal, but Anila slides it away from their striker and sends it back down the pitch. Karen's ready to take it and sweeps down the outside.

I roar with delight as she knocks it into the back of the net. Jeff's chewing on his pen, his eyes fixed on the play. With a minute to go, Treacle snatches the ball from a Westbury High defender and hammers it past the goalie. As she wheels away in delight, she gives me a wave. I wave back. With both hands! I'm so happy for her. I make sure I'm not standing too close to Jeff though. The last thing I want to do is ruin Treacle's moment of joy by making her jealous again. This playing Cupid thing is a whole lot trickier than it seems.

When the ref blows the final whistle Jeff throws his arms in the air and gives a massive cheer. 'I'll be celebrating tonight,' he tells me when he's calmed down.

'How?'

'Oh, I dunno – pizza and a Jack Black movie probably.'

Jack Black is Treacle's comedy hero! I knew it. The wedding cake is iced and the invitations are sent. I can't keep the grin off my face. A couple more nudges from Jessica Jupiter and these two will become one, I'm sure of it.

# 15

I have spent more nights in hospital waiting rooms than anyone I know. And here I am again, staring at the empty chairs.

Ben's fever shot up just after midnight and we had to bring him in.

You'd think they'd turn the lights down at night, but the waiting room's ablaze with a zillion fluorescent watts flaring like magnesium against the white walls and floors.

Mum's in with Ben. Dad's pacing the corridor outside. I can tell that he's torn between me and them. The nurses don't want us *all* in there.

'I'm OK,' I promise him. 'Go and sit with them. I've got my laptop.'

Dad stops and looks at me. 'Are you sure you'll be OK?'

'Yeah.' I've been here enough times before to know what to do. Whenever Ben gets an infection, I pack a bag with crisps, drink, chocolate, MP3 player, book and laptop and hang it on the back of my door when I go to bed. That way, I'm ready for any hospital waiting room anywhere in the world.

Dad reaches down and kisses my head. I don't really want him to go. I'm as scared as he is. But I swallow the lump rising in my throat and force a smile as he hurries away.

I reach into my bag and pull out the chocolate. Once a big chunk is melting on my tongue, I reach for my laptop. I might as well finish the horoscopes.

But once the document's open in front of me, it's seems silly.

Ben may die. I can't write dumb horoscopes for Jessica Jupiter. Instead I open a fresh file and start typing.

*When my brother was younger, he'd give everyone in the family a huge hug and a kiss before he went to bed. He refused to go to bed until he'd said goodnight to each of us 'properly'. One evening Mum asked him why it was so important to say goodnight 'properly'.*

*'In case I die when I'm asleep,' he told her.*

*My brother knows he has an illness which will never get better. It took us a long time to explain that he wouldn't die suddenly in his sleep, but we all know he will probably die before us. We just hope it's not soon.*

*Our family life is built around my brother. He needs a lot of care and therapy and exercise. We all take it in turns. Sometimes I forget I'm a teenager. Sometimes I forget I'm me. Sometimes it feels like I'm just his sister and not as special as he is.*

*I get tired of explaining to people that my brother's illness isn't catching. I get tired of having to keep the house clean so he doesn't get infections. I get angry when we have to cancel so many family outings because my brother's too ill. I get worried by my mum and dad worrying. And I get scared that if my brother does die, they'll be too sad to love me any more.*

*But that's on a bad day.*

*On a good day, our house is filled with love and laughter. Helping with my brother's therapy makes me a special part of a special team. And, because we all know life is fragile and that the world can be tough, we are kinder to each other than any family I know. My family doesn't just look after my brother, we look after each other. And we laugh whenever we can. I've learnt strength and courage from my little brother, and patience and love from my parents.*

*If you asked me if I'd change anything, I'd change only one thing. I'd make a cure for my brother because I don't want to imagine my life without him.*

I attach my article to an email, type in the webzine's address and send it from my hotmail account. Cindy will never know it's from me. My username's Newshound95.

'Gemma, love.' I look up and see Dad standing in front of me.

I catch my breath. 'How is he. Is he . . . ?' The words stick in my throat.

'He's stable.' I can hear relief in Dad's voice. It washes over me. 'I'm going to take you home so you can get some sleep.'

'What about Mum?'

'She's staying.' Dad takes my bag and swings it over his shoulder; then puts his arm round me and steers me towards the door.

Mr Harris clears his throat. 'I hope you don't mind if I sit in.'

It's Friday afternoon. Cindy's called a planning meeting for next week's edition.

I stifle a yawn, wishing I was home. It's been a long week. Mum's practically been living in the hospital, waiting for the antibiotics to start working. But so far, nothing's fighting the bug and Ben's still hooked up to machines with a round-the-clock watch.

I check my phone for the 498th time in case there's news, but there's no message icon flashing in the corner. I slide it back into my pocket and try to concentrate on the deadline meeting.

As soon as Mr Harris takes a chair beside the door, the door swings wide. Mr Harris ducks and Will rolls in like a thundercloud. 'No article from me this week,' he announces. 'My contact's pulled out, and with no interview, there's no story.'

'There's still the weekend,' I offer. I'm sitting behind

my usual desk, David and Phil opposite, Jeff leaning on their desk. 'Can't you find a new contact?'

'Yeah, right.' Will stares down at me. 'Like I'm tripping over stab victims.'

Sam's lolling in his chair, feet on desk. 'Hey, Will, any chance you could chill and give Gemma a break?'

Will flashes him a look, but shuts up. I give Sam a grateful smile.

'Don't forget Mr Harris has joined us today,' Barbara reminds us gently. She's sitting beside Cindy, smiling sweetly.

Cindy's not. Cindy's face is like stone. I guess she's trying not to crack her make-up. She and Barbara look like they're playing Good cop/Bad cop. I follow the fantasy, amused by the thought of Cindy drawing a Colt 45 out of her backpack.

'Sit down, Will.' I picture her pistol-whipping him into a seat, then wiping his blood from the muzzle. 'I want to get started.'

*I want to get finished.* Fear kicks in. Perhaps Mum's not texting because it's bad news. Perhaps I should just go straight home. I fight the urge to leave, reasoning that Dad would text me to come home if there was bad news.

'We need a lead article, Will.' Cindy taps her pen on her desk. 'Can't you pad out the info you've got?'

'Pad it out?' Will glowers at Cindy. He's perched on the back of his chair like the king of the vultures. The whole room knows there's no way he's turning anything in without tough facts, hard evidence and tight prose.

Mr Harris leans forward. 'What about using one of the articles submitted by the students?'

Cindy's jaw tightens. 'There's only been one this week, and I've not had a chance to read it.'

'Is it the document from *Newshound95*?' Phil points at his screen. 'Someone's saved it in the webzine folder.'

'Yes.' Cindy shifts in her seat. 'But how are we all going to read it? We still haven't had our printer installed.' She gives Mr Harris one of her icy glares. He looks at the floor sheepishly – like he's the pupil and she's the teacher.

'I have told the IT Department,' he stammers. 'I'll chase it up again tomorrow.'

'Dave.' Phil looks at his brother. 'If I send it to the printer in the IT suite, will you go and fetch it?'

As David nods, Phil does a quick headcount and starts mouse-clicking. 'I'll print one out for everyone.'

David heads for the door.

My heart's hammering. *Newshound95*. That's me. In three minutes everyone in this room is going to be reading my article while I watch.

I think back to last week's meeting: Cindy dumping every article sent in. Will's scornful critique of the school dinner item. I feel sick. I'm so not up to a round of mass criticism right now.

I resist the urge to plunge my head into my backpack and throttle myself with the zip. I decide that would probably attract even more negative attention than my article.

Jeff takes a comic book from his bag and shows it to Phil, grinning.

Phil's eyes light up. '*Watchmen*.'

'Original,' Jeff tells him.

Phil takes it and turns it over carefully, like he's handling a copy of the Domesday Book. 'It's the only graphic novel to be included in *Time* magazine's All Time One-hundred novels,' he breathes.

Cindy looks perplexed. 'There's a *comic* in the Top Hundred?'

Jeff scratches at a patch of Tipex on his jeans. 'Comic *book*,' he corrects.

'*Graphic novel*,' Phil re-corrects.

While they twitter in the background like the dawn chorus, my heart's thumping out a killer riff. I'm watching the door like a condemned man waiting for the jailer to fetch him for the noose.

David's footsteps start clicking towards the storeroom. Here comes the jailer. I put my hand to my throat. Who needs a noose? My throat's already too tight to swallow. My palms break into a sweat. As the door opens, I fight the urge to run. I steady my breath as David passes out the stack of copies in his hand.

Mr Harris takes one like a kid accepting candy. 'Is this the first reader submission you've had?'

'We had a couple last week,' Cindy answers briskly.

'But you decided not to print them?' Mr Harris asks.

'We had enough material of our own.' Cindy doesn't mention the mass-binning, but the memory is tattooed on my brain.

Numbly, I accept my copy. My hand trembles. I'm not ready for this kind of public scrutiny. I feel like a politician in a courtroom. 'A-are you sure there weren't any others in the folder?' I ask Phil forlornly.

'Just the ones from last week—'

'Hang on.' Mr Harris holds up his hand. He's already engrossed in the article. I scan the room. Will's reading; Jeff too. David's gaze is already near the bottom of the page. Sam's nodding his head as he scans his copy. Even Cindy's got past the first few lines.

'I like it,' she says, looking up.

I grab my chair in case I fall off. I'm shaking.

'It's great.' Mr Harris is flapping his copy. 'Who sent it?'

Cindy shrugs. 'The email just said *Newshound95*.'

Will sniffs and I glance at him, trying to ignore my heart hammering holes in my chest.

His gaze lifts off the page. 'It's *real*.'

'You like it?' I blurt.

He flashes me his 'ditz' look. 'Don't *you*?'

'Yeah.' I stare at my knees. 'Yeah, I like it.'

As my voice trails away, Sam speaks. 'I think it'll make a great lead article.'

Cindy's nodding. 'It ticks all the boxes. It's interesting, honest, well-written and inclusive.' She looks at Mr Harris. 'It really was a great idea to ask readers to submit.'

Wow. She's shameless. She hated the idea of reader submissions.

I wait for Will – Mighty Lord of Truth and Justice – to call her out. But he keeps his mouth shut.

Suddenly we're a team.

And my article's been accepted. And *not* because I'm the editor's best friend. Or because I'm writing easy-to-read trash. It's because Cindy, Jeff, Sam, David and Phil all like my work. Even Will likes it. Pride rushes through me, then stops dead.

I wrote this because of Ben. Because he's lying in hospital fighting an infection that might kill him. My article shivers in my hand.

I wish with all my heart that this success hadn't come from his suffering.

The sun is shining, clearly grateful that the clouds are letting it get a glimpse of the Cup Final.

I feel sadness twitching in my chest. Ben should be here, warm in the sunshine, helping me cheer Treacle on, not stuck in a hospital bed fighting for breath, his temperature spiking.

It's Friday after school and a soft wind is rippling the pitch. Parents, cutting work early, crowd the sidelines. Savannah is on the other side of the pitch hovering by Jason Brown, a Year Ten boy who is one of today's linesmen. He is also Definitely Datable and the perfect antidote to Josh. I'm standing in my usual spot. Jeff is next to me, hands in pockets. I'm glad he's here. He doesn't know about Ben. And that feels good. Because just having him standing beside me, like there's nothing wrong, makes me feel like everything is normal.

'Where's your notebook?' I ask him. 'Aren't you writing a match report?'

'Don't worry,' he assures me. 'I'll remember every move.'

Green Park High hasn't been in a final for years. The

Year Nine girls' team is the talk of the school. I even overheard Treacle's name mentioned in a corridor yesterday – by people who don't even know her.

Treacle's huddled with Karen, Jing-Wei, Anila and the rest of her teammates on the far side of the pitch.

I check the opposition. The Stavely Grammar School team are warming up in their half. They're all about six foot tall. Green Park are going to be stampeded by a herd of supermodels.

'They don't look like Year Nines,' I whisper to Jeff.

He grins. 'Perhaps they sent the basketball team by mistake.'

Nerves flutter in my stomach as the players fan out. For a moment I forget about Ben. Treacle's face to face with the Stavely captain. She's calling the toss.

'Did we win it?' I ask Jeff.

As he shakes his head, the ref blows his whistle and the Stavely centre forward punts the ball to her teammate.

I remember playing footie in the back garden with Ben. It was so cold that day. Is that what made him ill?

*Germs make you ill, not weather.* As Mum's voice echoes in my head, Stavely hammers towards goal. Treacle's been outpaced by a winger who gets the ball down the side and knocks it forward. Annie Hale, our goalie, gets a hand to it, but fails to keep it out. I groan: 1–0 to Stavely.

It feels like the end of the world. I take out my phone and check in case it's beeped a message alert. Mum promised she'd text if Ben's condition changed.

No message.

I force my attention back to the match, one hand wrapped round the phone in my pocket. I want it to buzz. But what if it buzzes with bad news? I'm as tense as a guitar string by the time Treacle takes a corner, firing a fierce side-footer which leaves Stavely no chance. Hope fires through my heart as Jing-Wei knocks it in and levels the score.

Ben will be OK. He has to be.

Stavely makes the first foray forward in the second half. The striker reaches the edge of the box and passes the ball. Her teammate loses control. Karen knocks it clear.

*Yes!*

I find myself pressing close to Jeff, the excitement almost too much to bear. If we win, Ben will be OK. His temperature will go down and he'll be OK.

But what if we lose? I stop making wishes.

Savannah runs to collect the ball and throws it to Jason. Somehow she makes it look as if she is performing a perfectly choreographed dance manoeuvre. Jason seems suitably impressed. I look back at the players. Treacle's red-faced and puffing, never still for a moment, her eyes following the action.

Suddenly I catch my breath, heart dropping like a stone. A Stavely forward swings a cross forward. Her teammate meets it with a header that clips Annie's glove and sails over the line.

I look at my watch. Five minutes to go and Stavely are one goal up. Green Park must be exhausted, but they push harder than ever. It feels like they're fighting for Ben. Go, Green Park! Treacle drills a low effort into the arms of Stavely's goalie. The goalie sends it back up the field, but Anila's hammering towards it and steals it from the Stavely defender. She dribbles it back down the pitch. Treacle's yelling for the ball, poised at the edge of the box. Glancing up, Anila passes, Treacle takes the ball and crosses it to Jing-Wei who slices it into the back of the net.

The crowd roars like it's Wembley and the ref blows his whistle.

'Penalties!' I catch my breath, trembling as the teams stumble to a halt.

'Worse than that,' Jeff murmurs. 'Sudden death.'

*Sudden death.* I can hardly breathe. Whoever gets one goal up first, wins.

On the other side of the pitch Savannah links arms with Jason. Treacle's bent double, her long black pony-tail sweeping the grass. Hands on hips, she gets her breath back.

The players stretch and pace at the centre of the

pitch. I can feel their nerves as their coaches start picking players for the penalties.

Miss Bayliss points to Jing-Wei, then Anila, then Treacle.

I grasp Jeff's arm. 'What if she misses?'

He puffs out a long, slow breath and shakes his head, not answering. He groans in dismay as Stavely get their first penalty in.

Jing-Wei squares up to the ball and backs off. With a short, sharp run-up, she lobs the ball into the back of the net.

I'm hanging off Jeff's sleeve like a kid, hardly breathing as the Stavely captain lines up for her penalty. Annie's in goal, arms stretched like an eagle, eyes fixed on the ball. The Stavely captain shoots wide and misses! I swallow back a cheer, my gaze fixing on Anila. If Anila gets this one in, we've won the Cup.

She places the ball and walks away, clenching and unclenching her fists.

Then she turns and runs. Her kick fires the ball forward and sends it sailing over the goal.

*No!*

It's still 1–1.

Treacle's pacing the goal, watching Stavely's striker take position.

I can hardly stand still as Annie manages to knock Stavely's attempt clear. They've missed again.

*Come on, Treacle!*

She puts the ball on the spot and backs away. I see her eyeing the goalie, then the net. Suddenly she rushes forward, her boot striking the ball with a satisfying thump. It soars through the air, brushing the tips of the goalie's glove, and lands smack in the top right corner of the net.

The perfect penalty and we've won the match.

And the Cup!

I throw my arms up and yell. 'We won! We won!' Grabbing Jeff, I jump around him like a deranged chimp. He's punching the air. Half the crowd is roaring with triumph. They start streaming on to the pitch.

I let go of Jeff and head for Treacle. Savannah gets to her at the same time and the three of us jump up and down in a group hug like three demented Tiggers. 'You were brilliant!' I gasp.

Her face is shining. 'Not bad,' she grins.

'Not bad? You're a star!' Savannah cries.

Jeff appears beside me. 'Fantastic penalty,' he says to Treacle.

She's still beaming. 'I can't believe it!'

Her teammates swarm round her, hauling her away towards the changing room.

'I'll wait for you!' I call over their heads.

Then I stop. I've forgotten about Ben. I was so caught up in winning, I forgot. Guilt rushes at me. I shouldn't have let him slip away like that. Panicking, I check my phone.

No message. Why did I stop thinking about him?

'Are you OK?' Savannah asks. I can see Jason hovering behind her, talking to Jeff.

'I'm fine. It's Ben.'

Savannah instantly looks panicked. 'Have you heard from the hospital?'

I shake my head. 'Mum said she'd let me know if his temperature went down, but I still haven't heard anything.'

Savannah grips hold of my hand.

'Savannah, are you coming?' Jason calls.

She looks at me. 'Do you want me to stay with you?'

'No, it's fine. You go with Jason.'

'Seriously, if you want me to stay, just say.'

'But what about Jason?'

'He's just a boy.'

That's why I love Savannah. She might be too cool for school, but she's never too cool for her friends.

I give her a weak smile. 'Honestly, I'll be fine. No news is good news, right?'

She smiles back at me. 'Right. Well, if you're sure?'

'I'm sure.'

'Promise you'll call me if you do hear anything?'

'Promise.'

Savannah heads off with Jason and as the crowds thin, I pace the sideline.

Jeff's hanging around too. He's holding his notebook. 'I want to get some quotes from the players for the article,' he tells me.

Before I can answer, my phone beeps. My chest cracks with fear. I pull my phone out, only half wanting to read the text.

*Please don't let him be worse.*

'Are you OK?' Jeff's staring at me.

I read the text.

*Fever gone. Ben sitting up, eating.*

'Yes!' I throw my arms into the air as if we've won another Cup.

'What?' Jeff's staring at me like I *am* a deranged chimp.

'Ben's better!' I'm actually jumping for joy. I *have* to jump or I'll explode with happiness.

Jeff waits for me to calm down. 'Who's Ben?'

'My brother,' I blurt. 'He's got cystic fibrosis. He's been in hospital with an infection since last week. But he's started getting better.' I feel like crying as relief swamps me.

Jeff blinks, his blue eyes suddenly bright. '*You* wrote that article!'

I nod. Tears are pressing harder behind my eyes. *Ben's going to be OK.*

Jeff cocks his head. 'Are you all right?' The kindness in his voice tips me over the edge. Overwhelmed, I start to cry. I feel Jeff's arms go round me and like a caring big brother, he gives me a hug.

*Ben's going to be OK!*

'What is going on?' Treacle's voice makes me freeze.

I back away from Jeff. 'N-nothing,' I stammer.

Treacle's face is set like stone, her eyes flinty hard. She drops her overflowing kitbag and spikes me with a stare. '*Oh, really?*'

I need a plan!

Treacle's on the verge of a major eruption and Jeff is about to make the toe-curling discovery he's been named her Man of the Century.

OK, here's what I have to do:

*First: Shut Treacle up.*

*Second: Calm Treacle down.*

I take a deep breath and say the magic words. 'Ben's better.' This stops Treacle in her tracks.

'Better?' Her eyes immediately light up and she hugs me hard. 'Gem, that's great.'

'I was just telling Jeff about him,' I explain.

Treacle grins as she realises why Jeff was hugging me. Then her smile freezes. I can read her expression like it's flashing headlines. She's realising that she's just thrown a jealous hissy fit in front of Jeff. Her gaze creeps nervously towards him.

Has he noticed?

I remember my research: this boy does not read between the lines too well. It was pretty amazing he worked out it was my article, but surely he won't guess that Treacle's head over heels for him just because she asked me what was going on?

*Will he?*

Jeff's rubbing his nose thoughtfully.

'You dropped your bag.' He reaches for Treacle's kitbag. As he grabs the handles, the football shirt spilling out of the top slithers on to the grass. 'Here.' He scoops it up.

Treacle reaches to grab it, but Jeff's staring at the number ten on the back.

'Wait . . . you're number ten!' he says slowly, like he's finally understood calculus.

I stop breathing. Is he thinking of his horoscope? *The number ten holds the key to your happiness.*

'Yeah.' Treacle hesitates. 'I'm always number ten. It's my lucky number.' She looks freshly scrubbed from the shower, her newly washed hair gleaming in the sun. She's not wearing any of the 'girly' clothes or make-up that she's been trying out, but that obviously doesn't matter to Jeff.

I see a blush spreading from the back of his neck, up into his cheeks. Slowly, he lifts his long, pale lashes and looks at Treacle. Then he smiles. 'You must be hungry.'

Treacle raises her eyebrows.

'Do you want to go into town and grab some pizza and celebrate your win?' Jeff asks her.

She looks at him like he's holding out a present, but

she's not sure if it's for her. She turns to me. 'Do you fancy it, Gem?' She doesn't see Jeff's face fall.

But I do. 'No thanks,' I tell her. 'I need to go and see Ben.'

'Oh.' Her brow furrows. 'Do you want me to come with you?'

I shake my head. 'No, you go and celebrate.'

Treacle shrugs apologetically at Jeff. 'Is it OK if it's just you and me?'

He pushes his hair from his eyes and looks straight at her. 'That would be great.'

And finally, Treacle gets it. This gift's definitely got her name on it, and hers alone. I want to hug her but I shove my hands in my pockets, not wanting to give the whole game away to Jeff.

Treacle glances shyly at her feet. 'OK.'

Jeff shoves her number ten shirt into her kitbag and swings it over his shoulder. Then he stands to one side to let Treacle pass.

She hesitates. 'Will you be OK, Gem?'

'Yes,' I say with a smile. How could I not be OK? Ben's better. Treacle's happy. 'I'll be fine.'

I watch her and Jeff trekking towards the gate. They're deep into match analysis by the time they disappear from my hearing.

Jeff and Treacle are going on a date. And my horoscopes helped make it happen!

I look at my watch. There's half an hour before the next bus to the hospital. Plenty of time to answer the rest of Jessica Jupiter's fan mail. Then I can spend all evening with Ben and Mum and Dad. I glance hopefully at the school building, wondering if the webzine HQ will still be open. It's late. It may be locked.

I see the caretaker over by the bike shed. He's holding a pot of paint and a brush. I cross the playground and stop beside him.

'What are you doing?' I ask, nodding at the paint pot.

'Just giving the old place a bit of a makeover,' he replies.

'But why, if it's going to be knocked down?'

He dips his brush into the pot and stirs it around. 'Haven't you heard? The powers that be have decided to keep the old place after all.'

'What?'

'Yep. Apparently, some article by one of you lot made them change their mind.'

My head starts to spin as it tries to digest this latest piece of information. 'An article?'

'Yep. In that new worldwide internet magazine thingy.'

'The webzine?'

'That's the one.' He lifts his brush from the pot and paints a gleaming streak of black across one of the railings.

'But I – that article was my idea.' I am smiling so hard now my jaw has actually started to ache.

The caretaker stops painting and his wrinkly face breaks into a grin. 'Well, good for you,' he says. 'Good for you. This shed's been here since I was a boy. Place wouldn't be the same without it.'

'Wow,' is all I can say. Today is starting to feel like my birthday, Christmas and Easter all rolled into one.

I glance towards the school. The windows are glittering in the sinking sunshine. 'Would it be OK for me to go back inside – to the webzine HQ? I wanted to finish off some work. Is the storeroom still open?'

He nods. 'I haven't locked it yet. There's another kid in there.' He looks at his watch. 'Gotta lock up in twenty minutes though.'

'I'll be done before then,' I promise.

Inside the school the corridors seem weirdly empty and bright. I take the stairs up to the webzine HQ two at a time and reach the door wondering who the other 'kid' is. It's probably Cindy stealing ideas from the bin, or Will following up leads.

I'm surprised when I hear music. I poke my head round the door and find Sam, leaning back in his chair, strumming a guitar.

'What do you think?' he asks as I walk in.

'About what?'

'My new song.' He strums another riff.

I smile. 'It's pretty.'

He grins and starts playing again. 'Thanks. I'm not sure I was aiming for "pretty" though.'

When Will says stuff like that, it's edged with razor blades, but there's no sharpness in Sam. I switch on my PC. 'Sorry.' I swing my hair over my shoulder. 'But it does sound pretty.'

He pauses. 'What's up with you?'

'Nothing. Why? Does something seem up?'

'No, you just look really happy,' he comments. 'You've seemed quite down all week. It's good to see you smiling again.'

I didn't think anyone on the webzine had noticed. 'My brother's been sick,' I tell him. 'But he's fine now.' Joy bubbles through me like I swallowed a bath bomb. 'And Treacle just scored the winning goal in the Cup Final.' I don't tell him that's not the only thing she scored. I'm not going to tell anyone till I get the after-date analysis from Treacle. 'And – I just found out that they won't be knocking down the bike shed. Cindy's article made them change their mind.'

'*Your* article,' Sam says, putting down his guitar. 'This is brilliant. We have to celebrate.'

I click open the latest webzine horoscopes to help me get back into Jessica's voice. 'What?' I look up, distracted.

'You and me.' He brushes his hair from his face

with the back of his hand. 'Why don't we go for a milkshake?'

I focus on the screen. I'm not sure how easy it will be to get into Jessica's voice when all I want to say is, *Ben's better*, over and over again. 'What?'

Sam gets up and comes to stand next to me. 'Oh, please don't tell me you have to consult your horoscope,' he says, looking at my computer screen and laughing. 'The whole school seems to think their life depends on Jessica Jupiter and her crazy predictions.'

A blush ambushes me. I pretend to look for something really important in my bag.

'All right then, let's see what yours say.' He leans over my shoulder. 'What's your sign?'

'Libra,' I squeak, trying to coax my face back to a normal temperature.

He starts reading from the screen. *'You may feel the scales haven't tipped in your favour this week. But don't fret, Star-ling. Good fortune will be linked to a young man with a three-letter name.'*

I glance up from my bag. He's looking at me, grinning broadly.

'A three-letter name, eh? Well that decides it.' He goes to his desk and starts putting his guitar back into its case. 'You've got to come for a milkshake with me. It's written in the stars.'